Dodge City By Lamplight

And How Wyatt Earp Fought A Dark Evil

By Carol L. Jenkner

This is a work of fiction. All characters and events portrayed in this book are either products of the author's imagination or are used fictitiously.

Acknowledgements

I would like to thank the following people for their help in getting this novella ready to publish. For their keen eyes and wise suggestions, I want to thank Gary Spencer and Roger Myers. For submitting artwork for a cover, thank you to Marilyn Black and Steven Flanders. As always, a big thank you to Pamela Gafford Maisano, my former English teacher and editor. She always encourages me with kind words and wise suggestions for improving my work.

Prologue

Throughout the era of the Old West or the Wild West, there were horrors recorded by daily newspapers. These events, if true, were often recorded weeks or months after they happened, were frequently elaborately embroidered to boost readership, and became legends that continued to be repeated.

Native Americans, like the Plains Apache, were blamed for acts of violence out on the empty prairie where there were no witnesses to verify the tales of vicious massacres. Where there were known murderers present, they were blamed even if no one saw them actually involved in a killing.

The Bloody Benders of Southeastern Kansas, a family of serial killers, Doc Holliday, Billy the Kid, and John Wesley Hardin were all accused of killings that were not their handiwork, although they had plenty of killings attributed to them that they willingly admitted. At no time were these gruesome and bloody massacres considered to be the work of supernatural entities. Only one man knew the truth.

Wyatt Earp was a living legend by the time he left Dodge City, Kansas. His fame grew with each Western town he entered. He was frequently hired as a lawman to keep the peace in towns such as Dodge City where cowboys flocked at the end of the Texas cattle drives to enjoy the pleasures of a wide-open town. By the time Wyatt Earp reached Arizona, he was a man who saw good and evil as black and white; the law was the law and he was there to enforce it. But in Tombstone, even he crossed a line in pursuit of justice, taking the law into his own hands and relentlessly pursuing and killing those he saw as his enemies. But even before he began the law enforcement career that came to define his character, he confronted a dark shadowy evil that pursued him until his death.

Chapter 1
The End of the Season

A cold wind rattled down the deserted streets of Dodge City, blowing dead leaves and bits of debris ahead of it. Huddled against the cold he crept along the rough boardwalk. The full moon, cold and silvery, cast shadows darker than the night itself. The streets were empty save for a stray animal or two, a cat running for cover, an owl calling in the distance along the river. It was a chilly night signaling the end of a summer full of the sights, sounds, and smells of a profitable cattle season. Fall was upon the land and headed for a cold winter if one could believe the predictions of the old-timers.

The shrouded figure heard the voices of men rising and falling over games of chance in the saloons along the street. Occasionally, the sound of a woman's voice rang high above the voices of the men; sometimes he heard the shrill scream of fury or astonishment when men got rough with one of the weaker sex. Off in some distant crib, probably back in Tin Pan Alley behind the saloons, the protests of a woman in distress, undergoing the brutal handling of a drunken cowboy, could be heard. Out on the prairie, a coyote's howl rent the night, startling horses safely housed in stables about town. Homeless curs slinking about the streets in search of a meal responded, barking and howling to the call of the wild.

The loan figure paused in the shadows watching the street, listening, waiting. He was patient, seeking prey of his own, nose pricking with the scents of dead and rotting animals, dung, sweating men, and spoiled food. His hearing was acute as was his night vision, both of which were needed to secure what he sought, what he needed to survive, this creature of the night. Hunting was easier in a warmer climate. Here everyone stayed inside when the days grew shorter and the nights grew colder, houses tightly shuttered against the winter chill.

Suddenly, he was alert. There was some slight movement in the shadows at the end of the street. He smelled the earthy richness of human blood making his body tingle with anticipation. He continued to watch for the movement he'd seen from the corner of his eye, but saw nothing. *Probably the wind,* he mused. He heard a sigh then detected another slight movement and lowered his gaze to see a figure struggling to rise against the corner of a building two blocks away. He felt the change come over him and suddenly, he sprang along the board walk, feet barely touching the ground, running as fast as the wind toward the helpless figure. Men looked up from card games as the dark shadow passed, setting lamps flickering in the smokey rooms. Hearing nothing, they returned to their games assuming it was simply a stray gust of wind. A terrified scream tore through the night then, bringing every man to his feet to rush for the doors. Lanterns were snatched up and lighted, guns unholstered as men swept out into the dark night in search of the source of the scream.

One man stood taller than the others, a natural leader. He stepped quickly to the front of the small crowd of men standing nervous and alert for a repeated scream, peering about with lanterns held high to light the ground about their feet. The tall man raised his head, listening and inhaling the air about him, seeking some clue to the direction he needed to go and fearing what he knew he was going to find.

Wyatt Earp, known far and wide as a skilled lawman, was calm under pressure, steely eyes staring down adversaries until they either backed away with downcast eyes or made the inevitable foolish move to pull a gun. His moves were cold and calculated, leaving nothing to chance. When he faced an enemy, he had already made up his mind that he would not be the one to die.

This latest threat to the people of Dodge City was something new, it was not a drunken cowboy, or a cold-blooded gunman like his old friend Doc, nor was it an angry gambler, losing at cards and desperate to win. He'd caught the scent of this creature before and never forgot what it left in its wake. He'd never seen the thing, but he knew in the deepest recesses of his soul that it was out there and that it was a creature from the depths of Hell.

what it left in its wake. He'd never seen the thing, but he knew in the deepest recesses of his soul that it was out there and that it was a creature from the depths of Hell.

Chapter 2
The End of Innocence

The Earp family was in Iowa when the Civil War began and Wyatt was thirteen years old. When the elder Earp brothers, Newton, James, and Virgil, left to join the Union Army, the younger boys, Wyatt, Morgan, and Warren, were left to handle the farm work. At thirteen, Wyatt felt he was old enough to go to war with the older boys and ran away several times to enlist. Each time his father tracked him down and brought him home. It was evident that Wyatt was not going to grow into the type of man who could settle down and work a farm or tend a business. Near the end of the Civil War, Wyatt's father moved his remaining family, including James who returned home severely wounded in 1863, to Southern California where Virgil would later join them.

The move and Virgil's return opened a new chapter in Wyatt's life. At sixteen he began working with his brother as a teamster and was soon given a route of his own hauling supplies to rail heads where he learned the art of gambling, an occupation he would return to again and again in his adult life. It was also during this time that he began to hear strange stories whispered around the cooking fires of railroad employees.

He automatically dismissed many of the barely understood tales of the Chinese workers as being foolish superstition. These Chinamen with their strange singsong language and foreign habits were viewed with suspicion by most white workers who ridiculed them and feared them. To Wyatt, they were an interesting group of people and he watched them in their quaint clothes adhering to their customs and rituals in spite of strange surroundings. He didn't understand a lot of what they said in their broken English, but he thought he got the gist of it. The stories seemed wild and too often associated with men disappearing in the night. Foremen assumed these men had run off, tired of the hard work and long hours, but Wyatt detected fear in men's eyes as they huddled around the cooking fires at night talking among themselves.

Many of the white workers were Irish immigrants and Wyatt initially discounted their wild stories, too. As a nondrinker himself, Wyatt viewed their drunkenness with distaste and suspicion. The Irish were a rough and violent group of men made more so by consumption of large quantities of alcohol. They were a loud and boisterous counterpart to the quieter Chinese, but they, too, seemed afraid.

In and out of the camps at varied intervals, it took Wyatt several months to make a connection between the stories the Chinese told and those of the Irish. But all of the tales involved the disappearance of men in the night, men dismissed by foremen as lazy runaways. On one trip, Wyatt found himself stranded because of a broken wagon wheel that forced him to spend the night at one of the more isolated camps. After sharing dinner with the foreman, Wyatt walked about the camp in search of a good cup of coffee. He found several likely sources and sat to sip the proffered coffee and listen in on campfire conversations. At one site, the conversation centered around home and family until the call of a distant coyote caused the men to look up and cross themselves with the sign of the cross. Wyatt asked why a coyote's howl had them all so frightened. Every eye turned toward him and one man began to tell him the story.

As near as the men could figure, one or more of their original group had disappeared each month around the time of a full moon. At first, the men did not make that connection, but simply accepted that a man had wandered off or run away. But as the months passed, the rail work progressed, and men kept disappearing in the night, they became suspicious of darker forces at work. One of the men thought he saw a wolf silhouetted against the evening sky, another reported a large cat, and still another thought he'd seen a giant bear. Soon they noticed that disappearances coincided with a full moon and the distant howl of an animal. They made attempts to report the incidents and requested an investigation but each time they were rebuffed and told to get back to work.

His interest piqued, Wyatt made an attempt to follow up by checking with other groups in the camp. He heard the same stories every time. The animal sightings varied, but the stories were basically the same. Counting the months and number of groups, noting the names of those believed to be missing, the number that had disappeared was staggering. He continued to make inquiries at each railroad camp and found that there were even more stories of men going missing. In a few cases where there were temporary towns that had sprung up, women of the night had also disappeared. Seeking to make sense of what he heard, Wyatt began to speculate about what was going on; he approached people he knew to be in law enforcement and asked if they had heard of gangs who might kidnapping people into slavery. It appeared the people disappearing were of so little consequence that no one cared.

As he moved in and out of the railroad camps, Wyatt continued to listen and watch his surroundings. On several occasions he spent the nights in a camp keeping watch to see if he could detect anything out of the ordinary that would account for the disappearances. And on a soft spring night in 1868 he finally caught sight of something that left his heart pounding with fear, a feeling he was largely unaccustomed to.

He had stepped away from the campfires to look at the full moon and wide expanse of stars across the night sky. A faint breeze from the south signaled the beginning of spring and brought a strange scent with it. Wyatt dropped to the ground, stilled his breathing and kept absolutely still, smelling the air and surveying the barely discernible horizon for signs of movement.

Off to his left, he caught movement out of the corner of his eye. Slowly turning his head and then his body, he watched and waited for the movement to occur. The scent grew stronger and the hair on the back of his neck stood up. Then he heard breathing, similar to a low anticipatory growl. He eased his gun out of its holster and raised it slowly, moving it left to right, watching for any slight movement. Then it happened, it was so fast it caught him unaware. Firing his gun was purely a reflex gained through countless hours of practice. The creature, for that's the only way he could think of it, was gone as quickly as it had come. He was sure, however, that he had hit it.

The next morning, he was up with the first rays of the sun searching for any sign that what he'd experienced in the night was real and not some bizarre dream. He found large prints resembling those of a wolf and traces of what he believed to be blood, confirming that he had hit the beast. Little did he know that his reflexive shot in the dark would torment him for many years to come.

Chapter 3
A New Beginning Brings Anguish

In 1868 the Earp family returned to Iowa from California and then moved south to Lamar, Missouri where Wyatt met and married his first wife, Urilla, in 1870. Things were looking up and Wyatt found his calling when he was appointed to a constable's position. He purchased land outside the city limits and built a simple home for his wife and their soon-to-be-born child.

Wyatt reckoned he was happier than he'd ever been in his life and had all but forgotten about the creature he'd encountered on a dark night in the spring of 1867. The little house went up quickly with help from his family. Urilla soon turned the structure into an inviting home for her husband and their unborn child. Living rough on the prairie as he had been, having a wife and comfortable house to come home to, made Wyatt more thankful than he imagined possible. Every day he thanked the Lord in his quiet way for the turn his life had taken.

Life as a constable in a small town was not a demanding job. He quickly came to know almost everyone in town, soon learned who the public drunks were, which men were prone to abusing their wives, and the men he could depend on for back-up if needed. Although more than proficient with his firearm, Wyatt preferred to settle differences without having to kill anyone. At six feet two inches tall, he towered above most men and hard work had given him a lean strength that made him a fearsome opponent when provoked. Even the meanest drunk soon learned to steer clear of the young constable. Wyatt quickly grew accustomed to the rhythms of the town. Payday would usually see a sharp rise in drunk and disorderly complaints as well as violence against women. He was thankful days like these occurred only once or twice a month because he hated coming home so late after Urilla, tired from her pregnancy, was already asleep.

She was a good wife, though, stoic and uncomplaining about the occasional late hours he was forced to work. She was proud of her husband and viewed him as standing between the good people she knew and the evil she suspected was out in the world. She loved him with all her heart and felt lucky to have married such a fine man. His drink of choice was coffee; he rarely touched alcohol because he felt he couldn't afford a loss of self-control. If someone had asked her, Urilla would have said his worst fault was gambling and even that usually put food on the table rather than taking it away as was the case of many men who could not resist the lure of gambling and money. Wyatt wasn't much of a churchgoer, either, but if pressed, he would escort her to Sunday services and smile doing it. He was also a generous man and others knew he could be depended on to help out those in need. His generosity would be his undoing.

As her pregnancy began to draw to a close, and the birth of their child drew near, Urilla began to complain uncharacteristically of strange things. At first, Wyatt chided her for her sudden fears, thinking they were a result of protective instincts due to the coming birth of their child. He was usually successful at calming her and getting her to laugh at herself for her silliness in detecting strange smells and shadows she could not account for. But within a day or two she would begin to complain of strange things again. She could not be specific when describing what she heard and smelled, but one day she described hearing a low growl, and he remembered his own experience years ago. He was suddenly afraid in a way he had never been afraid before.

It was about this time that he began to hear rumors of men disappearing, going out of town for a week but never returning. He didn't take it too seriously; men left their families, traveling salesmen were lured elsewhere to areas where sales were better, and men died of natural causes while away from home.

But how he wished he'd paid closer attention! He should have remembered those years driving wagons filled with supplies to the railroad camps. He should have remembered that night when he shot wildly at something that made the hair on the back of his neck stand up. If he'd thought of all of this in time, lives would have been saved and his life would have been filled with love and joy and children. It was all about to come rushing back making him regret his past curiosity about the disappearances of anonymous men.

At the end of a long day, Wyatt was sitting in his office waiting for the night constable to take over his duties when he heard yelling and the sound of running feet pounding past the jail. Getting up and going to the door, he thought to himself, *What fresh hell is this?* He called out to a man rushing past, "What's going on?"

The man paused and said, "Wyatt, come on! Your house is on fire!"

Wyatt started forward in stunned disbelief. As he moved, he picked up speed until he was sprinting past everyone. In the distance he could see the smoke rising from the direction of his house. The horse drawn fire wagon rushed past him, bell clanging. Rounding a slight bend in the main street, he was confronted by the sight of his home engulfed in flames. Without thought he pushed his way through the throngs of people and into the burning structure. He heard people shouting behind him, but ignored everything except his instinct to get to Urilla. As the structure began to collapse around him, he stood like a fiery demon shouting her name.

Hands grabbed him and dragged him from the conflagration, slapping at his clothing to put out fires caused by embers falling around him. One of the men said, "Wyatt, we got her out! Can you hear me!" Rough hands shook him, bringing him to his senses.

"Where is she?" he croaked.

A gentle hand took his arm and pulled him away from the others. He looked over to see his brother, a look of sorrow on his face. "Wyatt, we got her out, but it doesn't look good. She's over here..."

She lay on the ground under the shade tree behind their house. Although someone had covered her with a quilt, Wyatt could see that she'd bled a lot. Looking at his brother, he asked, "She lost the baby?"

Virgil just shook his head and then said, "Wyatt, it's worse than that. She's dying but not from the fire. She was attacked and left for dead then a fire was set to cover it all up. My God, Wyatt! Who hates you so much that they'd do this to your wife?"

Wyatt had seen a lot of bad things in his life, but never anything like what had been done to Urilla. Although her beautiful face was marred only by soot from the fire, the rest of her body looked as though she had been viciously attacked by a large animal with sharp claws and teeth. It was hard for him to look at her, but he forced himself to examine her so that he would never forget this day and what had been done to take everything he loved from him.

It appeared the unborn child had been ripped from her. He didn't have the heart to ask if the baby had been found or had even survived. The marks on her arms suggested she had seen the attack coming and attempted to fend it off. The marks on her thighs suggested something far worse. It pained him to think of her helplessness. He should have been there.

Urilla was still breathing when he took her poor savaged body in his arms. Amazing to him was the fact that she apologized for what had happened to her. As he smoothed her hair back, he soothed her as best he could. But she insisted on telling him something important.

"Wyatt," she whispered, "a man, it was a man at the door. All he wanted was some water. I turned away to get some water for him and when I turned around, he wasn't a man. I saw a beast where the man had been. I tried to get away, I tried to protect our baby..." She began to cry weakly as he hugged her closer and told her it wasn't her fault.

It was his fault and he knew it. It all went back to that night in the railroad camp when he shot wildly and hit something that he never saw clearly. But he never imagined in his darkest dreams that it would come after him. He still didn't know what it was and the one person who could have described it lay dying in his arms, now fainted from loss of blood and pain. He recalled Urilla's claims that she had heard things and smelled strange smells. He remembered how he'd laughed off her fears as the imaginings of a pregnant woman. How he wished he'd taken her seriously. *Could he have prevented this? Or would they both have died?* Urilla sighed and was gone, gone to a better place, he hoped.

He allowed his family to take over as he stood and walked away, walked toward the burned-out house looking for any clues. He was filled with the need for vengeance and he would have it. By God, he would have it!

Chapter 4
Fort Gibson, Indian Territory

Wyatt Earp remained in Lamar, Missouri for two years after the death of his wife and child. He did not share his suspicions with his family although his brother, Virgil, who had seen the horrors of war, knew something unexplainable had occurred with the death of Urilla.

Wyatt's grief was relentless and it showed in his behavior. He lost his job as constable, distanced himself from family and friends, and made a series of destructive decisions that would color his reputation the rest of his life. He went from a good life and a respectable profession to a partnership in a brothel on the edge of town. Although never accused of drunkenness, he could be found on occasion stumbling about town in a stupor, as though sleep walking through his own personal nightmare. He took up with whores and gamblers and his life continued to slide out of control.

He woke one morning to find his latest whore had left his bed in the night and disappeared. He was closely questioned about her disappearance. No one had seen her go, her meager belongings were left behind. The town was whispering about strangers in the night and strange smells. Conversations turned to the death of Urilla and the unusual details surrounding it.

The young woman was found a week later by Wyatt himself. Dead, of course, because death now seemed to follow him. He had gone to visit his wife's grave, a habit he had developed when he was troubled. He could be seen in the distance by others, sitting by her grave, talking quietly, gesturing as he would have done if she were alive to hear him.

As he approached his wife's grave he saw an unexpected and revolting sight. Instead of the pristine white marble stone of Urilla's grave, he saw the surface, stained with the dull rusty red of dried blood. Instead of bright flowers lovingly planted at the stone's base, there was a pile of dirty rags. Wyatt knew that the rags would prove to be the body of the missing prostitute, unceremoniously dumped at a site that was guaranteed to hurt and enrage him. He could smell the ferrous smell of spilled blood and decay of human remains. And there was another smell, too. He recognized it as slightly sulfurous, like the odor of a match being struck mixed with the smell of burning hair.

He was torn between alerting authorities, suffering the whispers and suspicions of the townspeople, or running away. He did the right thing, the thing his wife would have expected, and took off to alert the town constable of his unfortunate find.

He was not arrested for the prostitute's death. The vandalism to his beloved wife's grave prevented suspicion of Wyatt as a suspect. It woke him up, though, and he knew it was time to move on. He realized he needed a plan that would draw the evil that appeared to be following him away from friends and family, a plan that would lure it out into the open so that he would know what it was and how best to attack it. It would be a lifelong pursuit of vengeance.

By the end of 1869, Wyatt was at Fort Gibson, Indian Territory working as a buffalo hunter across the prairies of Texas, Indian Territory, and into Kansas. Trouble soon followed.It was December when Wyatt arrived at what was left of Fort Gibson. At one time it had been an important fort. Founded in 1826, it had been decommissioned and redesignated as a supply fort. A small contingent of soldiers, part of the U.S. 6th Infantry, maintained the fort and interacted with the surrounding Indian tribes in the area. One of the soldiers was a young private by the name of John Smith.

But, Wyatt never met the young man. He was already dead when Wyatt arrived at the fort. Soldiers were mustering a search for his killer or killers, assumed to be a small band of discontented local Indians who periodically made forays into that area.

According to the story Wyatt heard, the young man had been seeing an Indian girl and made it a habit to visit her at night when he could leave the fort. The morning after one such trip the private was missed when his horse came back to the fort without him. A detachment of soldiers went out in search of the missing man and found him dead along the trail near an outcropping of rocks that served as a local landmark. The report stated that he'd been shot in the back.

Wyatt witnessed the military burial shortly after his arrival. It struck him as odd how some of the men were behaving as their comrade was being buried. There was a lot of foot shuffling and sidelong looks. A few crossed themselves and appeared to be praying. In and of itself, this was not suspicious behavior; people prayed at funerals all the time. People got restless at funerals. People were uncomfortable at funerals. But there was something else that Wyatt couldn't quite put his finger on; there was an air of disquiet, almost like fear. These were seasoned infantry and there was no reason for them to be afraid of a death at the hands of a few renegade Indians.

A soldier that caught Wyatt's eye, a short man who stood in the back and slightly apart from the others. He held his head down and appeared at times to be weeping. Wyatt determined to get a little closer because there was something strange about the small soldier, something that piqued his curiosity. Out of respect for the deceased, Wyatt stayed still, but watched, waiting for an opportunity to move. By the time the brief service was over, the soldier had disappeared into the crowd of taller men heading back to their duties.

A month passed and Wyatt was in and out of the fort working with various outfits hunting buffalo. Every time he returned to Fort Gibson, he looked for the small soldier, still curious about him. He was told the young man's name was Thomas, Private Thomas; no one seemed to know his first name or anything about him.

As Wyatt got to know some of the soldiers, he'd join them in a game of cards now and then when he returned to the fort from a hunting expedition. He found that if he wanted information, this was a good way to get it. Men were a lot more likely to talk, even about the things they shied away from, when their tongues were loosened by alcohol. Alcohol was banned on the grounds of the fort, but that didn't mean men didn't have their bottles of medicinal alcohol secreted away. Others found ways to hide jugs along the banks of the river, retrieving them when there was a need. Wyatt stuck with coffee and gently pried information out of his fellow card players.

During one such card game, one soldier admitted that although Smith had been shot, his body had been savagely mauled by the time it was found. It hadn't been done by the renegade Indian warriors, if in fact they had even been involved. It appeared to have been done by a large cat with large claws and fangs. The body had been viciously ripped and chewed. The scalp and face were left intact and there was little blood, a fact that left the post surgeon puzzled. Also puzzling was the fact that big cats were rarely scavengers, not interested in things that were already dead. The level of ferocity of Smith's death left some of the more superstitious men frightened. Wyatt felt a tingle of apprehension, too.

In January, Wyatt was at loose ends and hung around the fort looking for work. This gave him more opportunities to watch the small soldier he had noticed at the funeral of Private Smith. As he watched it became obvious that Thomas often secretly slipped away late evenings or early mornings. Wyatt determined to follow him.

On his first attempt to track Private Thomas it was clear Thomas sensed he was being followed. He paused, listened, and then changed course, going to a secret jug stashed along the river bank where he took a deep drink before doubling back and returning to camp. Wyatt lost the slight young man on his second attempt to follow and sat in wait for him to return. But Thomas did not return in the way he had left and Wyatt spotted him the following morning at muster.

Wyatt's third attempt occurred on a cold, moonless night when the wind was blowing a gale, pushing ragged storm clouds across the sky. There was a definite scent of snow in the air. Conditions were perfect for following someone unobtrusively. Wyatt waited, freezing in the January night and was about to give up when he saw movement at the corner of Thomas's barracks. The young man crept furtively away from the building, his heavy coat pulled close around him. Satisfied he was not being watched, Thomas made his way toward his goal and Wyatt, keeping well back, followed.

Thomas moved like a shadow through the trees along the riverbank. Sometimes it was hard to tell the difference between the living man and the shadows created by the wind-tossed trees. Wyatt stopped short when the man paused then moved slowly forward out onto the sacred ground of the post cemetery. Under cover of the trees, Wyatt watched as the young man sought the most recent grave, that of Private Smith. He fell to his knees, his head bowed, hands pressed to his face. Wyatt thought he caught the sound of sobbing. He dared not move any closer and remained frozen in place wondering at this bizarre behavior.

He stood silently pressed against a tree and gradually became aware of a shift in the air around him. The wind stilled and the sky began to clear to reveal a full moon riding high above the earth's horizon. The scent of sulfur assailed his nose. Instinctively Wyatt shrank closer to the tree and stilled his breathing. He sensed what was coming but was still caught by surprise. He expected to see something show itself, but instead he saw the young private lift his head and stare at the moon. He seemed to grow in stature, slowly rising from his kneeling position and turning to meet something unseen. Out of nowhere a black cloud formed and flung itself at the young man out on the open grave site. Although he saw clearly, Wyatt still could not make out what was happening; it was over quickly and left death in its wake.

Wyatt continued to watch, taking great care to remain silent and out of sight of the thing still hovering over the downed soldier. He could not tell what the creature was; it appeared to him shadowy, amorphous, and lacking the definition that would signal a specific animal. Perhaps, after all, it was a human covered in dark clothing and wearing a hood.

Finally, it raised its head and Wyatt got the impression of a snout that trembled, snuffling the air, and looking about in all directions. Was it a wolf after all? Fortunately, the wind was blowing toward him, and carrying his human scent away from the animal that stood over the soldier's body. Then it vanished; in one minute plainly visible and in the next gone. It gathered itself and with a flash, disappeared.

Chapter 5

Arrested

Once he believed himself to be alone, Wyatt stepped from the cover of the trees, striding toward the figure on the ground. The wind had calmed and all was stillness around him. The odor had also gone leaving Wyatt feeling confident that he was now alone. When he reached the prone figure, he stooped to check for any life, expecting none. This creature had not left behind the damage to the body that had been done to Urilla, but the clothing had been ripped and torn and the face slashed.

Wyatt got slowly to his feet and stared down in horror at the body, not that of a young man, but a young woman. Why had he not seen this before? Was he so far gone that he could not determine the differences between man and woman? As he stood over the body, sadness at what he had witnessed overcame him and he bowed his head in an uncharacteristic prayer for this young woman's soul.

He was suddenly aware of the sound of approaching men and horses. Before he could react, a small detachment of soldiers, perhaps returning from some errand, came into view. Wyatt hoped that in the darkness they would not see him and would ride on to the fort. Luck was not on his side. One man spotted him and alerted his commanding officer.

The soldiers turned and rode toward him, taking in the dark scene as they drew near. Wyatt was encircled by men and horses with no way to escape. He said hoarsely, "Private Thomas was a woman!"

Caught off guard, several men dismounted to take a closer look. The officer in charge spoke to Wyatt, "Did you kill her?"

"No, Sir, I did not!" cried Wyatt. "I spotted Private Thomas leaving the barracks and thinking it an unusually late hour, I followed to see what he was up to. I lost him, but found him again when I heard sobbing. I was astonished at the sight of the young man crying over the grave of another dead soldier, so I watched. When time passed and I saw no movement, I walked over to take a closer look and found the soldier dead and in this condition."

Every eye turned to look at Wyatt. Every eye took in the dead woman with her shredded clothing and scratched face. Every eye turned to stare at Wyatt with a look of utter disbelief. "I find your story disturbing," said the officer. "I do not believe you. How is the clothing so torn and the face scratched if you only followed her to the dead man's grave?"

"I do not know," said Wyatt, loudly. "As I watched, a fog arose and swirled over the graveyard, I heard sobbing, and when the fog lifted and was gone, I saw the soldier slumped over the grave. When I checked on him, this is what I found." Several men quickly crossed themselves..

The officer, however, was not of a superstitious nature. He simply saw a man standing over a dead soldier whose appearance suggested he had been roughly handled before he had died at the hands of the man in front of him. "Arrest this man!" he cried.

Rough hands grabbed Wyatt, his hands were firmly tied with a rope and the rope tied to a saddle horn. The officer shouted a stream of orders to the other soldiers under his command. One of the soldiers had been given the job of placing and securing the body across his saddle. He grumbled at having to walk while leading his horse with its burden while others rode.

By this time, no one was paying much attention to Wyatt and he waited for an opportunity to escape this predicament. He appeared to stumble and fall, drawing the attention of the soldier to whose horse he was tied. Jumping from the horse's back, the soldier reached out to jerk Wyatt to his feet, a compassionate act that cost him the suspect. Wyatt was on his feet quickly and had possession of the man's pistol before the man knew what was happening. He ordered the man to untie him, then with gun in hand, ordered the others to remain still or he would shoot the officer astride his horse. With the horse as his shield, Wyatt walked toward a line of trees, jumped into the saddle, and was gone. He called out as he rode away, "I'm sorry, but I am not taking the blame for what I did not do." He sped away into the trees to make himself less of a target.

The confused soldiers looked to their officer who was quickly off his horse and stamping his feet, shouting expletives. Regaining his composure, he motioned the detachment forward and headed them toward the fort.

The disgruntled hunting party reached the fort where the officer threw his reins to his sergeant, shouting, "Take care of my horse!" and went in search of the fort's commanding officer. He turned back abruptly and said, "And take that body to the hospital!"

Within the week, a more efficient detachment of soldiers had found and arrested the unfortunate Wyatt Earp for murder and horse theft. He was thrown in the guardhouse joining two other men arrested for stealing horses.

It didn't take long for the three prisoners to talk among themselves, providing Wyatt with valuable information about his surroundings and the barely manned fort. Wyatt waited for an opportunity to escape. The talk mostly centered on the death of the young soldier, now discovered to have been a woman he was accused of having killed.

Wyatt's companions in the guardhouse were accused of horse theft, although both proclaimed their innocence declaring mistakes had been made. The first man brought before the judge was acquitted in spite of the complaint lodged against him by the wife of the second man. She declared in her testimony that her husband had been forced into the crimes he had committed. When the second man was called before the judge, Wyatt decided he wasn't waiting around any longer.

At just over six feet tall, Wyatt had an advantage and he clawed his way to freedom through the low ceiling and poorly built roof of the guardhouse. He determined to make his escape on foot rather than risking another charge of stealing a horse. He stayed away from the roads going in and out of the fort instead keeping to the trees and a shallow creek.

Once far enough from the fort, Wyatt managed to catch a ride on a farmer's wagon after offering to work both for the ride that took him into Kansas and for the extra horse the man had won in a poker game. The wily farmer had hired on as a teamster hauling goods from the fort, now a commissary site, to other locations during Reconstruction. He left his wife behind to run the farm while he made some much-needed extra money. On this trip he was headed north to the nearest railhead at Baxter Springs in Kansas. The farmer, named Abner, was no fool and guessed the tall young man was running from some trouble at Fort Gibson, but he was a man on a mission to increase his land holdings and the extra pair of hands would work to his advantage.

The talkative farmer, Abner, explained that he'd been to the fort conducting business, playing cards in the evenings to pass the time. He said he won the horse during one of these nightly games. He remarked slyly, "Those soldier boys didn't put up much of a fight. All they talked about was two dead soldiers. Some of them were afraid, talking about strange events surrounding the deaths. The others were discussing the disappearance of a suspect." He looked sidelong at Wyatt, a speculative look on his face. "You wouldn't know anything about that, would ya?"

"I know that I wasn't involved," said Wyatt ending the conversation.

Wyatt had hired on to work and work he did! Abner roused him at sunrise and expected Wyatt to be engaged in the hard physical labor farmers were accustomed to until sundown. Abner was surprised at Wyatt's knowledge of farming and assumed the young man had likely been raised on a farm somewhere. "You work on farms before?" Abner asked.

"I've done lots of things to earn my way," explained Wyatt. My father was a farmer, my brothers were soldiers, and we've all driven wagons to earn our way. I know hard work and I don't turn away from it."

Abner loved to talk, relating a constant stream of gossip and only falling silent when he ran out of things to say, or when Wyatt moved away from him. Never much for conversation, Wyatt listened, but said little. He was thankful he had escaped the fort before Abner had arrived. It would have been just his luck that the one wagon he'd seen in days belonged to someone who recognized him and fancied himself a bounty hunter. He guessed Abner had his suspicions, but wouldn't act on them because he needed the extra farm work done.

It was clear that spring was coming. The air was softer and there was a hint of green along creek banks nearby. He was suddenly looking forward to the horse and freedom he'd been promised. He even stayed on a little longer than asked in order to finish the work that needed doing. Abner paid him fairly explaining that his sons had taken up homesteads some distance away and had not yet returned to help with spring planting.

At loose ends, Wyatt was unsure what direction he should take. He lay out under the stars one night after work was done for the day, weighing options. Always in the back of his mind was that niggle of fear that the creature that had killed Urilla was still with him, following him. If that was even remotely true, Wyatt had no desire to bring that evil into his family again. He felt as though Urilla's horrible death was somehow his fault although he couldn't really define his reasoning. All he knew was that somehow, through his own curiosity, he had attracted its attention.

Had Wyatt listened to his small inner voice, the one he thought of as Urilla's voice, he would have stayed in Kansas and avoided the trouble he was about to face in Peoria, Illinois. Peoria was a bustling city along the banks of the Illinois River. He thought about it, knowing that Morgan and his wife Lou were there running a profitable saloon and brothel. But when Morgan and Wyatt got together, there were always schemes and doubtful decisions.

Chapter 6
Morgan's Dream

Many miles to the north, Wyatt's brother, Morgan, the youngest of Wyatt's brothers, was something of a happy-go-lucky braggart, living more off the earnings of his wife's prostitutes than off his own saloon. He was the exact opposite of his older, more introverted brother, more impulsive, more prone to loud talk and drink, but when they got together all bets were off.

It was unusual, then, that Morgan went to bed one night and fell into a dream, the like of which he'd never experienced. It was frightening to him even after he was awake and knew it to be only a dream. It left such a profound feeling of fear that he wrote it down intending to share it with Wyatt the next time he saw him.

In this dream, Morgan saw his brother walking through flames leaving the burning house he had lost when Urilla died. He saw something lurking behind Wyatt covering him in a dark fog. As Wyatt moved toward him, away from the flames, there was a look of terror on his face and he tried to tell Morgan something. Wyatt cried and yelled but still, Morgan could not hear him. He strained forward trying desperately to hear and understand until Wyatt was within inches of his face and Wyatt screamed, *"Run! Run for your life!"* and all the while, Morgan heard laughter as the darkness enveloped Wyatt and he completely disappeared.

Morgan was unsteady and shaking when he finally got out of bed. His wife, Lou, was still fast asleep and he left her knowing her nights were often longer than his. He went to the basin to wash his face, toweled off, and dared to peer at himself in the wavy mirror above the table. His face was white and drawn, his eyes bloodshot and with horror he realized there were faint scratches across his face, already beginning to fade. He stepped back and looked over the rest of his body. There were also fading scratches across his chest and abdomen. *What the hell?* he wondered. *What had Wyatt gotten himself into?!*

Chapter 7
Wyatt In Peoria

Wyatt began a period of wandering aimlessly, gradually working his way north, unsure of exactly where he was headed or what he wanted to do with his life. He was still grieving the loss of his wife, their child, and the good life that might have been. Without thinking he began edging toward Milford, Missouri where Urilla was buried. He had trouble finding the grave because it had too long since he had visited it. Guilt rolled over him like a giant wave. When he finally found the site, he saw that someone was at least keeping the weeds pulled away from the stone and there was evidence of some flowers laid there at some point.

He slowly dismounted and sat in the grass on the grave. Head bowed, he began to pray that Urilla had gone straight to heaven and was living her eternal life there in peace and beauty. He sat for a long time talking to her as though she sat on the sofa in their parlor in front of him. He told her how he missed her, wondered whether they would have had a boy or a girl, and discussed with her how happy he would have been to have a little girl that would grow up to be like her mother. He ached with every fiber of his being for what could have been.

When he stood to leave Urilla's grave Wyatt sensed he wasn't alone and looking around saw a woman watching him. He assumed it was one of Urilla's sisters, but made no attempt to approach or talk to her. He turned and led his horse out of the cemetery and began his aimless journey in and out of Kansas and Missouri. His wandering took him into the new cattle shipping points in eastern Kansas. He worked his way from town to town visiting gambling houses and engaging in games of chance. Occasionally he encountered people he knew, but stayed away from his family. Scarcely knowing why or how, Wyatt found himself back in one of the towns of his youth, Peoria, Illinois, where he found his younger brother Morgan with his wife Lou.

Wrenched by guilt and grief Wyatt fell into further debauchery in Peoria.

The man who would become a legend became a bouncer, gambler, bartender, and a pimp, running a keel boat along the shores of the Illinois River near Peoria. He became so worthless a human being that he spent countless nights in jail, arrested for running a bawdy house and for beomg drunk and disorderly. He came to be known as the Peoria Bummer.

And then the real trouble began. Prostitutes began to disappear much as they had after Urilla died. No one thought much about it if a prostitute was reported missing by one of her fellow practitioners and pimps rarely put themselves on the spot reporting a missing girl. It did not go without comment among the sporting crowd, though, especially the madams who kept close eyes on their stables of working girls. Lou began to report that some of her girls were followed and threatened by someone who kept to the shadows so the girls could not see them, but they heard them and felt the presence of some menace.

It became Wyatt's job to keep an eye on the girls and escort them if needed. He, too, became aware of the presence always out of sight, always in the shadows. He began to carry his pistol, something he rarely did. At this time, he had one special girl, Sally, who shared his bed most nights. One morning he woke to find she had left some time in the night. He didn't think much about it because Lou often called on the girls for chores around the house.

Her absence was remarked on by the end of the day because not only had Wyatt not seen Sally, but no one else had either. It wasn't like her to go off without saying something to Lou. By ten p.m. the local constables were banging on the door of the brothel demanding to know who was in charge and where Wyatt Earp could be found.

Lou acknowledged that the house was hers and asked what the police wanted. "May I know what this invasion of our privacy is all about?" she asked.

"Do you keep a woman here named Sally?" asked a burly policeman.

"I have a woman who boards here by that name," replied Lou, "but she has been gone all day on some private matter of her own."

The constables knew that her ravaged body had been found in a distant corner of Peoria's Springdale Cemetery where the tall prairie grass and a lone Sassafras tree hid a circle of stones few were aware of. A white-faced groundskeeper had run to the police station to report his gruesome find, saying he rarely visited that area of the cemetery because it was largely unpopulated with graves. According to him locals referred to it as the demon's circle because of the desolation of the site and the forked leaves of the tree.

What the he described left the constables open-mouthed with disbelief. The groundskeeper drew a lurid verbal picture of a large flat stone covered in gore, blood-stained grass, and a circle of women's bodies laid round a central figure. All had been savagely attacked and killed then left for wild animals to further desecrate.

While out looking for Sally, Wyatt had found the place but quickly withdrew, trying to decide if he should notify the police or if he should simply abandon another town and head for a more desolate and unpopulated part of the country. He had no doubt this ugly scene was the work of the demon that pursued him. He hid in the overgrown grass behind a more distant headstone and heard the shouts of the constables as they approached. He dared not move, but heard their reactions loud and clear. The cries of horror and disgust, the sound of one man vomiting up his hard-earned lunch, were plain and painful to hear. Wyatt heard his name several times and knew that he was a target of law enforcement once again.

He knew he had to leave or he would end up at the end of a rope, either judged a heinous murderer or lynched by the good citizens of Peoria. He could only hope that the passage of time and the nature of people would erase memories of this crime he did not commit. He sneaked quietly away to claim his horse from its stable blocks away from the place he had been calling home and hoped that Morgan and Lou would understand. Maybe he would write them later to let them know why he felt he'd needed to disappear so suddenly and without a word.

Chapter 8
Moving On To Kansas

Still restless and weighed down by the guilt that was now a part of his life, Wyatt moved on to solitary pursuits he was more accustomed to. He spent some time with the Atchison, Topeka and Santa Fe Railroad as it pushed westward into Kansas. While working there, Wyatt met two men who would remain his friends for life, Bat and Ed Masterson. When railroad work grew scarce, Wyatt joined his new friends in buffalo hunting on the south-central plains of Kansas. It was hard, stinking, grueling work but it allowed little time for thought or self-pity.

It was during this time that Wyatt began experiencing the nightmare that would continue to plague him off and on for the rest of his life. He found sleep hard to come by and frequently prowled the hunting camp drinking coffee and smoking cigarettes that he expertly rolled one-handed. If he was honest with himself, he was awake and prowling because he feared the demon would come in the night and take one of his new-found friends. He was ever watchful, constantly sniffing the air for that sulfurous scent he associated with an attack.

Bat watched this activity for a while, night after night, before he decided to join Wyatt and see what demons kept the man pacing like a caged animal. Thankful for the company of a friend, Wyatt offered to teach young Bat Masterson about gambling. Years later, Bat would acknowledge that all his talents as a gambler were the result of Wyatt's teaching. But he admitted he never found out what kept Wyatt so on edge at night.

One night when Wyatt managed to sleep, he had a nightmare that left him wide awake and sweating. Wyatt watched his friends killed by a fiendish buffalo that seemed to take on human hatred and blood lust, goring and stomping the hapless hunters until they were reduced to a bloody pulp. Wyatt fired his rifle again and again but the bullets simply bounced off the beast. Wyatt braced himself as the buffalo turned to face him, a fiendish look in its red eyes. As Wyatt watched, the beast became a cloud of thick, black smoke and disappeared with a loud pop.

It was time to move on. As he continued to roam at night, watching and ready should something approach their camp, Wyatt considered what to do. It appeared that anyone who grew close to him was in peril. He determined that if he could not escape the peril, could not protect his family and friends from this demon, he would live the life of a recluse consorting only with the lowest elements of human beings. He listened to the talk among other hunters they met on the plains and decided that a raw and violent cow town was the best place for him to be. He vowed he would head for the current railhead and see what there was for a man in his prime, of dubious reputation, and who had a great deal of skill with cards and guns.

He heard that the cattle had moved west from Abilene, Kansas to a little-known town called Ellsworth, a town just on the brink of notoriety for its drinking, gambling, whoring, and cowboy violence. It was rumored to be a frequent residence of the likes of Ben and Billy Thompson, two brothers known for their skill with guns. And Billy had a troublesome temper to match.

As a new day began, Wyatt collected his earnings from Bat and said goodbye to the Masterson brothers. He headed for the greater excitement and violence of the newest cattle town in Kansas.

Chapter 9
Ellsworth, Kansas

In Ellsworth Wyatt stayed on the fringes of the crowds of cowboys streaming into town. He engaged in his usual pursuits in the gaming halls, worked off and on as a bartender and faro dealer. He never did anything to call attention to himself, but his skill with cards soon drew the admiration of Ben Thompson and the ire of his brother, Billy.

Billy was a mean drunk, quick to anger, quick to take insult, quick to jump up and draw his weapon. Ben, the elder of the two brothers, was an easy-going man who took responsibility not only for himself but for his younger sibling. Ben's restraining hand was about the only thing that calmed an angry and precipitous Billy down. So it was that when Wyatt began to win a lot of money from an increasingly drunken Billy, Billy saw an insult to himself and jumped up, pulling his gun as he did so.

Wyatt sat calmly, staring up at the red-faced young man in front of him, no older than Wyatt himself in years, but decades younger in maturity. "Someone get Ben Thompson," Wyatt said quietly. He did not want to have to shoot Billy and draw Ben's rage. "Can I buy you a cup of coffee?" asked Wyatt, trying to distract Billy and calm him down. "Drink some coffee and we'll play again if you want," urged Wyatt wondering where in the hell Ben was.

Ben Thompson was a big man and the crowd parted before him when he made a beeline for his brother. Everyone knew that Ben protected Billy and no one challenged that. "Billy," said Ben, "what's the trouble here?"

Billy turned with relief toward Ben and said, "This scoundrel has cheated me out of all my money! I'm just gonna shoot 'im and get my money back!"

"I don't think that's a good idea, Billy," soothed Ben. "This here's Wyatt. You remember him, don't you? We've admired how well he plays cards and never seen him cheat."

Now Billy looked puzzled. "Wyatt?" he asked. "He's our friend?"

Ben put a calming hand on his brother's arm. "I think we've had enough card playing for the night. Let's turn in and get some rest."

But this time the magic didn't work. Billy jerked away from Ben and continued to brandish his gun. "I'm not quitting until I get my money back, friend or no friend!"

Wyatt said the wrong thing. "Hey, Billy, what do you say I just give you your money and we can play another day?"

The enraged Billy saw only an insult in Wyatt's words and pointing his gun straight at Wyatt began to squeeze the trigger. He blinked when Wyatt's unseen gun took Billy's weapon right out of his hand. Suddenly Billy was looking into the barrel of an unexpected six shooter.

"Time to sober up, Billy," said Wyatt in a stern voice. "No more cards and whiskey for you." He got up to leave the table, taking his winnings, he nodded at Ben and said, "You can thank me in the morning." And he walked out to the admiration of every man in the saloon.

After that it was harder to keep a low profile, but no one made a move to mess with Wyatt Earp. A contrite Billy, his brother by his side, appeared in front of Wyatt the next afternoon and mumbled an apology for something he could hardly remember happening.

Ben took a long, hard look at the man in front of him and said, "Why don't you and I have a friendly game of cards this evening?"

"Sure," said Wyatt, "whatever you say." And he walked away, disappearing into the crowd of people on the street.

Wyatt joined Ben in the saloon late in the evening. Just the two of them played; Billy was not included and he sat nearby sulking and drinking. Ben had taken his brother's guns away early in the evening to avoid trouble later. As Ben had declared, Wyatt did not cheat, but he did know all the tricks from years of card playing. He knew Ben would cheat to win, and vowed that if he caught him, he would certainly call him out on it. The poker games dragged on with no one winning and no one losing.

Taking a break, Ben looked around to find that Billy had left them. He looked around the saloon expecting to see him at the bar or gambling in another part of the large smokey room. Not seeing his brother, he said something to Wyatt and got up to see if anybody knew where Billy was.

Meanwhile, Wyatt stepped out back to relieve himself. Moving down the dark alley, he rolled and lit a cigarette and leaned against the building to smoke, looking up at the starry skies overhead. All seemed quiet except the occasional sounds associated with night time in a cow town. Wyatt heard a shuffling noise and a low growl to his immediate right. A pair of large dogs were fighting over something.

He looked away wondering where Billy had gotten off to when he suddenly tensed and shrunk against the side of the building. That smell, familiar now and frightening. The smell of the creature Wyatt had encountered five or six times now reached his nostrils again. He looked cautiously over at the fighting dogs. They had drawn away from each other and from the thing they were fighting over, snarling and belly-crawling away from the object in fear. Wyatt heard raised voices on the main street and clearly heard Ben Thompson shouting at his brother Billy, asking what he had done. He sounded frightened.

The smell had gone by now and Wyatt stepped closer to see what the dogs had left. He gasped in horror when he saw the remains of a woman, torn and bloodied. He didn't recognize her, but what was left of her dress suggested she was one of the many prostitutes operating in the alleys behind the saloons lining this part of the main street.

He walked around the side of the building to see Billy standing in a circle of men with lanterns held high. Billy, with a dazed look on his face, stared down in surprise at the ax he held in his left hand. "I didn't do it!" he shouted drunkenly, but his blood-spattered face and clothing suggested he had certainly done something.

Ben was being held back from helping his brother escape another misdeed while the men surrounding Billy waited for the sheriff to arrive. Wyatt wisely stood back in the shadows waiting to see what Billy had to say for himself, but he appeared drunk or drugged to the point of incoherence.

The acting sheriff arrived and began asking questions. No one could tell him anything except that Billy had been wandering in the middle of the street holding the ax and covered in blood that did not appear to be his own. Billy continued to tell anyone who would listen that it wasn't him.

Wyatt stepped out of the shadows and moved toward Ben and the sheriff. "I think the victim may be in the alley behind this building," he said, gesturing behind him. I noticed a pair of dogs fighting over something and when I went to have a look..." He looked around at each man and continued, "Well, it ain't a pretty sight. If you have a weak stomach, I'd stay back."

The sheriff called for more lanterns and the group moved into the dark alley behind the saloon. The dogs were snarling over the remains again and had to be chased away. There was a collective gasp as the men approached the savaged body of the woman. Several men moved hurriedly away back out onto the main street. Billy had been taken to the jail where he could be watched and restrained if necessary, although he continued to move like a man deep in the grip of a drug-induced nightmare.

A sheet was found to cover the woman who was placed on an old door and taken to the doctor's office for examination. Cause of death was attributed to an attack by a large animal like a wolf, but no one had seen or heard such an animal in the vicinity. And that did not explain what Billy Thompson had been doing with a bloodied ax.

Ben was allowed to clean his brother up and bring him clean clothing, and then Billy was allowed to sleep off the drugs or alcohol he appeared to have ingested. Questioning began next morning when Billy woke up. As expected, he became belligerent when he realized he was locked in a cell. Ben was called in to sit with him as he was questioned.

"Billy," began the sheriff, "what happened last night?"

"I was watching Ben and Wyatt play cards," he said. "I was drinking and watching, but I got bored and decided to join another card game, but there wasn't an opening so I went outside."

"Maybe you wandered down to the opium den that Chinaman runs," said the sheriff.

"No," said Billy. "I don't mess with that stuff. I was drinking like I always do."

"Do you remember anything after you went outside?"

"Well, I...," began Billy. "I don't remember anything. Not one damned thing! I didn't think I'd had that much to drink."

"So, you don't remember killing a woman in the back alley of the saloon where Ben was playing cards," stated the sheriff.

"No!" shouted Billy. "I wouldn't do that." But he was puzzled at the lack of any memories.

What were you doing holding a bloodied ax and wearing these bloody clothes?" asked the sheriff as he held up the things Billy had been wearing.

Billy looked blank. "I wasn't – was I?" he said. He looked toward Ben and asked, "Was I holding that ax?"

Ben nodded. Billy looked frightened.

Ben said, "Try to remember something Billy, anything after you went outside."

Billy closed his eyes and tried to remember what had happened. His eyes flew open and he said, "I felt so tired. I started toward our rooms, but I heard something and I went to see what it was. A woman was crying and a voice whispered in my ear telling me to pick up the ax and take a swing." Billy looked at his brother, a terrified look on his face. "But I didn't, Ben, I did not kill her! Instead, I walked out into the street to get help." There was a long pause. "That's all I remember. It must have been the man who whispered who killed her."

The sheriff got up to leave the cell asking Ben if he wanted to remain with his brother. Ben declined saying he needed to go find Wyatt and see if the two of them could straighten this situation out. He was convinced by the obvious fear in his brother's eyes, that Billy had not done this terrible thing.

The sheriff shook his head and said, "He acts like he's gone stark raving mad."

When Ben found Wyatt and described the conversation in Billy's cell, Wyatt was already well aware of what had happened and that Billy was not involved, but he couldn't tell Ben or the sheriff that. They'd think he was crazy, too. But he agreed to talk to the sheriff on Billy's behalf and see if the Thompson brothers could be allowed to simply leave town on the condition that they didn't return.

When Wyatt gave his carefully edited version of what he thought had happened, the brothers were allowed to leave. A week later, after the Thompsons were well away from Ellsworth, Kansas, another prostitute was brutally murdered, exonerating Billy, but leaving the mystery of the killings unsolved.

Chapter 10
Nights of Introspection

Soon after the Thompson brothers left Ellsworth, Wyatt Earp decided it was time to move on. He knew by now that he could not escape, could not outrun the terrible thing that was always with him. He decided he had a taste for law enforcement and as the cattle trade moved to Wichita, so did Wyatt. His reputation as a cool customer and a gunman preceded him and it wasn't long after his arrival that he was approached by a group of city councilmen and interested citizens asking him to take a position as a policeman to help quell the problems with the cowboys coming into Wichita with the Texas cattle.

Before he arrived in Wichita, though, Wyatt spent days on the move sleeping rough on the prairies at night and moving at a leisurely pace during the day. On one particular night he found a place to camp in a grove of trees along a small creek. He built his camp fire, brewed some coffee. He had stopped for a meal at a way station and still had some biscuits that he'd wrapped up and stuffed in his saddle bag. He wanted to think about the life ahead of him He considered how he had acquired the demon that always seemed to follow him and what he could do to rid himself of it. Without really knowing anything about it or even what exactly it was made it hard to do anything to rid himself of it. How had he acquired this presence, this thing? Had it come after him simply because he had wounded it? Were there others? He reasoned that if it could bleed, then it could be killed.

On that thought, Wyatt lay back against his saddle and stared up at the vast sky full of stars overhead. Hours later he was awakened suddenly to feel someone lay down next to him. Although he knew in some corner of his mind that he was laying on the ground out in the open, when he turned to look to his left, he saw his sweet Urilla propped against one of her white pillows staring into his face. She looked just as he remembered her.

In the soft voice he remembered so well, she said, "Oh, Wyatt, what have you done?"

As he struggled to raise himself up on one elbow, he whispered, "I do not know, Urilla. Can you tell me what I am going to do about this? I don't even know what I'm fighting." His eyes filled with uncharacteristic tears and he said in a broken voice, "I am sorry for what I did to you. You did not deserve that. But I didn't know." He lowered his head and when he looked up again, she was gone and only the smell of sulfur remained with a whisp of black smoke in the air.

Wyatt lay back again, wide awake now and staring up at a night sky that was gradually lightening toward the dawn. He was beginning to question his own mental state, wondering why he was seeing a creature few seemed to sense and why he was now seeing the ghost of his late beloved wife. He was somewhat mollified by the fact that others before him had sensed the creature, but this didn't explain where it came from or what it was. Where had it come from? Had the Chinese laborers in the railroad camps brought it with them? Had the Irish? Or, as he had begun to fear, was it a figment of his own imagination that had grown out of those fantastic stories told by the railroad laborers?

The argument raged back and forth in his brain. If it was only his imagination, then why had Urilla died such a horrible death? Was it only coincidence that she had been attacked by some passing stranger who had gotten away with murder? Had Wyatt just linked it to his nightmarish encounters with something that may or may not have been real? He searched is brain for other answers. His thoughts were drawn to stories of the family of serial killers known as the Bloody Benders. Perhaps they were behind some of the killings. No one appeared to know where they were. Perhaps a roving band of Confederate marauders had murdered his wife. The problem with all of these explanations was that no one had seen or heard anything to suggest it had been a group of strangers in the area. Wyatt feared that he was going to live with these dreadful mysteries for the rest of his life, where periods of peace and forgetfulness would be followed by a reappearance of the creature and vicious killings.

In the meantime, Wyatt was headed for Wichita with the goal of disappearing into the crowds of cowboys. He hoped he would soon be entering the growing city that would hide him for a while.

Chapter 11
Wichita Lawman

Almost as soon as he hit town, Wyatt was hired by an acquaintance who knew his reputation for retrieving money owed. He was often called upon to escort wagons containing goods and money to ensure their safe arrival at various destinations. Eventually he was called upon to join the police force when his reputation in Ellsworth finally caught up with him. Wyatt was determined to stay clean and free of controversy, but at six foot two inches tall and handy with his fists or his gun, he was often the target of bad men and men who envied his reputation as a law man. At about this time, his brothers James and Virgil were also in the area with their wives, running saloons or acting as lawmen, but staying away from prostitution.

At this time, Wyatt had been introduced to Mattie and she would become his common law wife for a number of years. The problem with Mattie, though, was an addiction to laudanum and she kept a small bottle hidden in her pockets at all times. It had become such a problem that Wyatt never knew which Mattie he would come home to – the bright-eyed party girl or the morose sobbing woman. He urged her to get help, to give up this addiction, but she continued to deny she had any kind of problem. In trying to do right by this woman, Wyatt had once again made a choice that would cause him endless trouble. He couldn't even say he loved her, but only pitied her and Mattie hated it. She railed at him, accusing him of comparing her to Urilla, the blessed saint, screaming an ugly stream of obscenities until one night, Wyatt could take it no more and slapped her. He was immediately sorry for his action, but it seemed to sober Mattie up for a while.

Wyatt spent more and more time on the job and away from home to avoid Mattie, hoping she would eventually tire of his neglect and leave. But she did not. Wyatt had his hands full at work anyway, and gave her little thought only going home to sleep once in a while. If Mattie became unbearable, he was known to sleep in an empty cell or seek shelter at one of his brothers' places.

An altercation with his boss's rival landed him in trouble at a politically sensitive time and he was dismissed from the police force only to be hired back a few weeks later. No one questioned that he did a good job maintaining the peace in cow town Wichita.

Plagued as he was, Wyatt scarcely noticed the occasional disappearance of a prostitute or transient. Even missing cowboys did not draw his interest or attention until he was given the task of doing something about it. Many had simply died of drug overdoses, alcohol poisoning, gunplay, or had moved on to other places.

Then he was handed a very odd case to deal with. Two prominent city government officials had disappeared without warning or reason. One man had been found dead miles away, the one thousand dollars he was known to have on him was still in a hidden pocket where he had placed it. There was no evidence of foul play, no gunshot wounds, no bruises from a beating, no signs of strangulation. When he was examined as he was prepared for burial, the undertaker noted that it appeared his heart had exploded within his chest cavity. Someone suggested he'd been frightened to death, but there was no proof or sign of anything that might have frightened him. It was explained as death by natural causes and filed away.

The second missing man returned, but his wife stated that he was unrecognizable and obviously demented. The doctor was called and then the police. After examining the unfortunate man, the doctor noted that his clothes were ripped to shreds and bloodied, his hands and face were burned, and when his clothing was removed and the man placed tenderly in bed, the doctor further noticed the bottoms of his feet were burned as well. Perhaps the strangest thing of all was the man's inability to speak coherently. He made sounds, tried to talk to his wife and the doctor using hand motions, but it was all completely unintelligible.

The doctor bandaged his hands, left salves for his face and feet and instructed the wife in caring for the unfortunate man. She was given a bottle of laudanum for pain as he appeared to need it and instructions for preparing soft comforting foods in order to bring his strength back. It was hard to know exactly what to do for the man. His condition was a complete mystery to the doctor and policemen alike.

Upon hearing of the man's return to his home, Wyatt asked if he might visit him and see for himself the harm that had been done. He suspected he knew the source of the damage done to the man, but was completely unprepared for the man's eyes. The burns were healing, he still could not speak so that anyone understood, but his eyes told the story of some horrible mistreatment and unfathomable fear. He pleaded with his eyes for Wyatt to understand him and Wyatt did understand, but all he could do was sit with the man and ask him asking him questions that required a positive nod or a negative head shake

One day as he sat with the man, hunched forward, hands clasped between his knees, Wyatt asked the him, "Shall I pray over you? Would that help?'

The man looked at him with fear, but gave a nod. He tried to form words. Wyatt could see the struggle, see his lips trying to form the words he wanted and the tightness of his throat muscles as he strained to get the sound out. Words finally emerged, but were so strange that Wyatt assumed they were another language he was unfamiliar with. He called to the wife and asked her husband to try again, only to get the same result.

"Your husband speaks a strange language, ma'am," Wyatt said.

"He speaks English the same as you and me," she replied. "That's the same gibberish he's been saying all day. I don't understand it, but it sounds harsh and ugly. It must be some foreign language he's picked up in his travels."

"What does he do for a living?" asked Wyatt.

"He's county treasurer here," she replied. "Haven't they told you? He left here to take the train to Topeka on some state and county business and disappeared for weeks. I reported him missing, but he had vanished. He was happy and had one thousand dollars on him when he left. He was looking forward to the journey to the state capital but when he appeared at our door he was unrecognizable to me. Whoever did this to him didn't even steal his money or his watch or the ring he wears. It seems like he was battered for the sheer pleasure of seeing his pain." She began to cry softly as she stroked her husband's hair.

When she returned to the kitchen, Wyatt once again took the seat next to the man's bed and began to pray, but a strangled cry from the broken man before him stopped him. The fear in the man's eyes and the negative shaking of his head puzzled Wyatt. Most people in such a condition were comforted by prayer, but this man appeared to fear it. "I'll let you sleep, then," he said to the man. "I'll come back tomorrow to sit with you. If you can write, perhaps you can write down what you need, what I can do for you." He turned and left, saying his good-byes to the wife as he let himself out. He noted that she was making a cup of tea for her husband.

Wyatt hadn't gone far when he heard the crash of breaking china and a woman's scream. He rushed back, flung the door to the house open and moved into the kitchen. The broken cup was on the floor. There was sobbing from the adjacent bedroom. As he stepped through the doorway, he saw the man lying on the bed, blood coming from his mouth, breathing harsh, and his wife sobbing loudly. He looked at the man more closely and realized he held a razor in one hand and his own tongue in another. Eyes full of despair he slowly bled to death.

Chapter 12
Headed for Dodge City

Wyatt's brother Virgil showed up at the door of his room in a nearby boarding house the next day. "Wyatt!" he shouted, "What the hell is going on! The police are looking for you. They think you had something to do with the man who disappeared and then showed back up weeks later."

"I had nothing to do with any of that," said Wyatt. "Could you keep your voice down?" Wyatt stepped back to allow Virgil into his room and sat on the edge of his bed. "If the police want to talk to me, they know where to find me; I haven't left town. I'm not in hiding and I'm right where you'd expect to find me this time of day."

"They said you visited that man," said Virgil.

"Yes, and his wife was right there all the time," said Wyatt. "Why? Did she say something different, accuse me of something?"

"No, but what were you doing there?" asked Virgil. "Did you know him?"

"No, I just wanted to talk to him and find out what had happened," explained Wyatt. "Is there a crime in that? I was given the job of finding two missing men. One turned up dead, the other came back in such a state I wanted to know what had happened to him."

Virgil sighed and finally sat down. "I want to know what's going on with you," he said. "You haven't been yourself since Urilla died. In fact, I'd say you've been like a man possessed these last few years."

Wyatt looked up sharply. "Can't a man mourn his wife?"

"You're not fooling me, Wyatt," responded Virgil. "I know there was something wrong about Urilla's death. It wasn't natural the way she was torn up. I was the one who went into that burning house and carried her out. I could see she wasn't going to make it and she kept saying something I couldn't quite catch, but it sounded like she was trying to tell you something about a demon."

"You didn't think to tell me this before now?" asked Wyatt.

"You were so broken up and I didn't figure on adding some unintelligible gibberish to your pain," said Virgil. "But I can see by the look on your face, that you already knew all of this. What is happening with you? You've left every town you've been in with some kind of cloud over you and a string of very strange events seem to occur wherever you are."

"I'm not going to talk to you about this, Virgil," said Wyatt in a low voice. "It's better if you don't know about any of it."

"I'm your older brother, damn it!" exclaimed Virgil. "I want to help you, if I can!"

"You can't," said Wyatt, firmly. "I'm not going to discuss it further."

Virgil could tell by the stubborn look on his brother's face, that he wasn't going to get any information out of him. "Okay, then, is it true the man cut out his own tongue?" asked Virgil.

"My God, Virg, who in the hell does such a thing?" Wyatt said in an anguished voice. "I just wanted to see if he could talk to me and he tried, but it was just a bunch of gibberish, some language I'd never heard before. He couldn't write because his hands were bandaged. He looked so desperate. I finally asked him if he'd like me to pray with him." Wyatt paused then continued, "That poor man drew back from me like I'd hit him. He had such a look of terror on his face. I've never seen a man look so terrified at the simple mention of prayer. I finally told him his wife was coming with some tea and that I'd visit another time. I left him laying back on his pillows, his eyes closed. I spoke to his wife as I walked through the kitchen. She asked me to leave the back door open as I left. I assumed she wanted some air coming in. I wasn't five steps from the back door when I heard the sound of breaking china and her scream."

"And you ran back into the house?" prompted Virgil.

"Of course I did," said Wyatt," and I saw him laying there bleeding to death, a razor in one hand and his own tongue in the other. His wife had fainted. I ran for help, but of course he was beyond help."

Someone banging on the door to his room alerted Wyatt to the fact that the local police had arrived. He opened the door and invited the city marshal in. "What can I do for you, marshal?" asked Wyatt.

I've come to have a word with you about that man that cut out his tongue," said the marshal. "The wife says you was there visiting her husband. That true?"

"Yes," said Wyatt, "I just wanted to see if the man could talk to me and tell me what had happened to him. Is his wife saying something different?"

"No, but strange deaths seem to follow you and people are talking," said the marshal.

"Let them talk," said Wyatt. "If you're not arresting me, then I think I'm just going to pack my bags and move on. This place is suddenly getting too crowded for me." He stared the marshal down, daring the man to arrest him.

"No," the marshal said, "I was just hoping you'd have some answers is all. Moving on sound like a good idea, though." He put on his hat, nodded at Virgil and Wyatt and left.

"I hear Bat Masterson and his brother are in Dodge City," said Wyatt. I hear that place is hopping with cowboys bringing cattle in this year. Maybe Bat will put in a good word for me."

"Sounds like a good idea," nodded Virgil and he left Wyatt to gather his belongings and collect his horse before heading west.

Chapter 13
Dodge City

As Wichita grew the cattle trade moved west to Dodge City, a place frequently referred to as a wide-open town where cowboys ruled side by side with gamblers, prostitutes, thieves and saloons. Every pleasure that a tired and dirty cowboy could want was there. Shootings and killings were frequent and law enforcement needed extra help in the summer months. Wyatt had heard much the same about Fort Griffin in Texas, but he had friends in Dodge City, and he didn't know a soul in Fort Griffin. So, he showed up in Dodge City just as the season was beginning in 1876. His reputation preceded him and he was hired as a policeman assigned to night duty.

As he walked along Front Street most nights, Wyatt got to know just about every professional gambler, saloon keeper, prostitute, and general denizen of the night. He soon realized that something else lurked in the dark alleys; he could smell it. Until it showed itself, whatever it was, he couldn't do anything about it. It did not seem so focused on Wyatt as it had been, but it was pretty clear that Dodge City was a feeding ground. Most deaths in Dodge City went unremarked simply because there were so many shootings, far too many for the newspapers to keep up with. Lower class citizens such as the cheapest prostitutes and faceless unknown cowboys simply had no names in Dodge City and their deaths were not mentioned. Even screams in the night no longer emptied the saloons because there were so many.

But Wyatt examined each death as though it was something newsworthy, looking for new details to tell him something more about his adversary. It attacked unexpectedly catching its victims off guard. It ripped and tore at the victims and then ate its fill of their soft inner organs. After that it might be weeks before another attack. Wyatt tried to keep track of the attacks comparing them to the dates when there was a full moon. In spite of the rumors he'd heard in the camps out west years before, the phase of the moon did not appear to have anything to do with the attacks. The creature did not attack during daylight hours but only during the darkest hours of the night. Although it appeared to prey most often on women, it did not seem to care whether the victim was man or woman, adult or child when it needed a victim. Wyatt reckoned if it was hungry enough, it would eat just about any kind of meat, but it seemed to prefer humans.

No one in Dodge City had said a word about a monster killing and eating humans, no reports of missing people, no unexplained deaths; it puzzled Wyatt that the thing went almost completely undetected. He supposed it was because the Dodge City that operated by lamplight was a violent environment and had little connection to Dodge City in full daylight when the good folks went about their business unmolested. No one seemed especially concerned about the condition of the dead bodies, either. There were frequent reports of knife fights; prostitutes were often well known for their skills with knives, easy to carry hidden, slipped into the top of a stocking or the folds of a skirt. Many gamblers were also well known for carrying knives, as were buffalo hunters and trappers.

Ah, well, Wyatt sighed, *Dodge City was a violent city, especially after dark. Maybe people just took it for granted.*

As the cattle season began to wind down, Wyatt found himself without a job. He was assured he'd be hired again for the next season, but for now, no extra lawmen were needed. He decided to take a trip north and see what was going on in Deadwood. South Dakota. By all accounts it was a dangerous place where the gold fields kept a steady stream of gamblers and prostitutes in lwork. He'd heard someone had gotten the jump on Wild Bill Hickok, shooting him in the back of the head as he sat playing a game of poker. Bill ordinarily would not sit at a table unless his back was to a wall and no one could sneak up on him, but his carelessness this one time had gotten him killed.

That was also the summer General Custer was killed in a battle with Indians in Montana Territory at a place called Little Big Horn. Wyatt had never met the man, but figured his well-known arrogance had finally cost him his life and the lives of his men. The battle had been a total massacre.

Wyatt headed for the Black Hills, convinced he could make his fortune one way or another. In Nebraska he met his old friend Bat Masterson who was headed back to Dodge City. He warned Wyatt that the place was overcrowded with other hopeful miners trying to get rich before heading back south and winter closed in. But Wyatt stubbornly declared he was going ahead and he arrived in Deadwood to find things exactly as Masterson had told him.

Wyatt was till determined to mine the situation whether it was panning for gold or gambling for gold. He settled in for the winter. He knew the gambler's lifestyle and was comfortable with it, occasionally tending bar or acting as a bouncer when he needed to earn a few extra dollars. Knowing of his reputation, locals often called on him to settle disputes or assist with guarding a stage taking gold out of Deadwood.

After a few weeks he noticed there was no evidence that the creature had followed him north. Considering some of the conclusions he'd reached about the thing, Wyatt decided it did not like cold weather and after a harsh winter in Deadwood, neither did Wyatt. Soon the cattle season would begin and Wyatt wanted to be at the head of the line when Dodge City needed more law enforcement officers. The next week, in April of 1877, Wyatt left, headed back to Dodge City. Even without trying his hand at gold mining, he left the Dakota Territory with a tidy sum of money in his pockets simply because he knew how to provide the needs and services people were willing to pay for.

Chapter 14
Dodge City, 1877

Wyatt arrived back in Dodge City in early July as reported by the *Dodge City Times* of July 7, 1877. The paper spoke of him with admiration and Wyatt was pleased by the ready acceptance of his skills as a lawman. When Wyatt arrived, Bat and two of his brothers were there and working to rein in the cowboys' enthusiasm.

Wyatt was well-regarded in Dodge City. He had acquired another common-law wife the previous summer and set up housekeeping. Their life together was relatively quiet for a town like Dodge City. Wyatt had reached a place of uncommon peace of mind and thought perhaps he might gain the kind of life he'd had so briefly with Urilla.

He realized his mistake when he left for South Dakota at the end of the 1876 cattle season. Mattie refused to go, declaring that she was settled and of no mind to move. Wyatt left her behind, refusing to be manipulated.

By the time Wyatt returned to Dodge City for the cattle season in the summer of 1877, Mattie was again engaged in prostitution, her former profession. When Wyatt showed up at the door of the house he had bought for them, she simply remarked, "So, you're back." She left the door to the house open and walked away, declaring herself sick with a headache and going back to lay down.

Wyatt accepted the open door as the only invitation he was going to get. He noted the darkened rooms, untidy furnishings and bedding and half empty bottle of laudanum on the table beside her bed. "One of your bad headaches, Mattie?" he asked quietly.

In answer to his question, Mattie lay back on her bed, her back to Wyatt and said, "Bring me a damp towel."

There was no 'please' or 'thank you', but Wyatt knew how surly Mattie got when suffering from one of her headaches. Knowing she would not be pleasant company, he decided to go see a man about a job. He would return later and hope she was in a better frame of mind. He turned to leave and said, "I'm going to get my old job back. Send someone to find me if you need anything."

He had his hand on the doorknob when he heard her muffled voice, "Bring me another bottle of laudanum in the morning and you can move back in if you want to."

Wyatt refused to engage her in a battle of wills, knowing full well, as she did, that he owned the house and could put her out any time he wanted to. The truth was that he felt sorry for her.

Wyatt returned in the morning with the promised brown bottle. He looked at it with distaste. He hated the stuff. Their days resumed the pattern of last summer. He slept most of the day and worked at night. Mattie occasionally engaged in prostitution with a few favored clients, but often slept at night and well into the following day when the headaches came. She became increasingly addicted to the powerful opiate.

One morning, as the cattle season neared its end, Wyatt woke with a sudden fear. He sat up and looked around in alarm but breathed a sigh of relief when he saw Mattie sleeping peacefully beside him. He reached over to smooth the hair off of her face, checking to make sure she was really alive.

The dream had been so vivid. He'd been back in Lamar with Urilla. Life had been good; it had been peaceful and their child was coming into the world soon. Suddenly, Urilla's calm face had been replaced by Mattie's face twisted with loathing, pain, and fear as she struggled to breathe, clawing at the neck of her gown, eyes bulging. She was trying to scream; he could feel the effort she made to live, but as he watched, her eyes dimmed and the life left her. A shadow passed between them and suddenly he was awake and in the present.

Mattie stirred beside him and opened her eyes, staring, still under the influence of the laudanum. "Wyatt," she whispered, "is something wrong?"

He shook his head. "No, go back to sleep. I'll watch over you and keep you safe as long as I can." This would not be possible although he didn't know it them.

Chapter 15
Doc Holliday

As the hot, dusty summer eased into fall and the year's cattle season ended, Wyatt stayed on, too afraid to leave Mattie behind. She had dismissed his dream as a silly nightmare when he broke down and told her about it. Wyatt had planned to keep his promise to protect her, convinced the dream was a portent of her death. She simply waved him away as she took a small sip from the bottle of laudanum that was her constant companion.

The demands of law enforcement, however, had another plan for Wyatt Earp. When the gang of cattle rustlers and train robbers known as The Trio robbed a Santa Fe Railroad camp in southern Kansas Wyatt was appointed a temporary United States Marshal. He was sent in search of Dave Rudebaugh and his band. He tracked them from Kansas south across the Oklahoma Territory and into the region near Fort Griffin in Texas.

The trip ended in disappointment when Wyatt failed to capture Dave Rudebaugh and his gang. When he entered the town of Fort Griffin Wyatt headed for the Beehive Saloon where he knew the owner, John Shanssey. Shanssey said that Rudebaugh and his band of outlaws had been there, but had left a few days before,

"You just missed them, Wyatt," said Shanssey, "and I don't know where they were headed. That fella over there in the corner can probably tell you, though."

Wyatt surveyed the room, fixing on a well-dressed man sitting at one of the corner tables, sipping whiskey and absent-mindedly manipulating a deck of cards. "He a friend of Dave Rudebaugh?" asked Wyatt.

"No," replied Shanssey, smiling, "he just managed to win some big money off Dave and lived to tell about it. Name's Doc Holliday and he's damned quick with his gun or his knife. I think Dave left the table a little afraid of the man."

"Thanks," said Wyatt and sauntered toward the table where Holliday sat. Addressing the gambler, Wyatt said, "Howdy. Heard you might be able to give me some information about Dave Rudebaugh and his gang. Name's Wyatt Earp."

"Well," drawled Holliday, "aren't you a tall one! Sit down so I can see you better. I'm a little unsteady on my feet just now and don't fancy trying to rise to meet you formally,"

Wyatt smiled and took a seat opposite the man, careful to sit out of reach of a knife, taking Shanssey's warning to heart. "Friendly game of cards?"

"Sure," said Holliday smiling now, "let's see what you've got."

The two men played several hands of poker, sizing one another up before giving too much of themselves away. Holliday was frankly surprised by Wyatt's skill and calm demeanor.

"So," said the gambler after losing the last hand, "why are you looking for Dave? You a gambler he owes money to?"

"No," replied Wyatt quietly, "I'm a United States Marshal trying to find him and his gang. They robbed a railroad construction camp in Kansas."

"Judging by my experiences with him, you should be able to track him by smell alone." Holliday said smiling at his own joke. "He left here about four days ago. I overheard him saying he was headed back to Kansas to try his hand at robbing trains."

"Thanks," said Wyatt. "I'd like to stick around and win more money off of you, but I have a long journey back to Dodge City." He turned to walk away, then stopped and turned back to face Holliday. "You should come on up to Dodge City. It's a lot more exciting than this place."

Wyatt finished his business and headed back to Kansas. As he rode, he speculated on the strange man he'd just met. He instinctively felt they'd become friends in spite of Holliday's cold blue eyes and dangerous appearance.

Bat Masterson eventually caught up with Dave Rudebaugh and his gang after they tried to rob a train at Kinsley, Kansas. That attempt was foiled by an alert young telegraph operator, Andrew Kingkade, who leaped across the tracks in front of the incoming train as it neared the depot. Kingkade signaled to the engineer to pass on through and jumped on board out of harm's way. The robbery attempt was an utter failure and the would-be robbers rode away.

The slippery Dave Rudebaugh managed to escape jail time by turning state's evidence on his companions in crime. He was alleged to be committing crimes in New Mexico in April of 1878, but Wyatt was positive he'd occasionally see Dave's sly face in a crowded saloon or on the lamplit streets of Dodge City, but whenever Wyatt made a move to approach the man, Dave would disappear into thin air.

On the night of April 9, 1878, a tragedy occurred that left Dodge City stunned. City Marshal Ed Masterson was walking the streets on the south side of the plaza, chatting with friends in and out of the saloons. It appeared to be the usual orderly mayhem. Ed and his assistant entered the Lady Gay Saloon and noticed a couple of Texans carrying their pistols. Ed stepped forward and notified them that they needed to check their guns at the bar when inside the city limits of Dodge City. He relieved the men of their pistols, handing them to the bartender. Shortly after, the two lawmen left the saloon to resume their stroll up the street.

Not yet hired for the new cattle season, Wyatt was standing nearby when he saw two men come out of the Lady Gay, seemingly intent on Ed. He watched in horror as Ed turned sharply and attempted to wrestle the gun away from one of the Texans. Angry that the man had his weapon back, he lunged to take the pistol, but was shot as Wagner jerked the gun free at point blank range. The other Texan, Walker, held the deputy back, gun to his head. Panic ensued, Wagner was shot and killed, and Walker was crippled.

In the melee Wyatt heard hollow laughter and looked left to see Dave Rudebaugh beside him. "Got 'im!" said Dave and disappeared with a puff of smoke.

Wyatt looked swiftly around, puzzled by what he'd just experienced. In later years, long after he was able to defend himself, a rumor floated around briefly that gave Dirty Dave Rudebaugh the blame for shooting Ed Masterson. But Dave was a long way away and the only one who claimed to have seen him was Wyatt, admitting that only in his later years."

Chapter 16
Leaving Dodge City Behind

One more season in Dodge City and Wyatt Earp was tired of being a lawman and he was tired of Dodge City. He was looking to the West and dreaming about settling down and becoming a businessman.

Mattie was against the idea until Doc Holliday and his woman, Kate Elder, showed up in Dodge City. The two women disliked one another on their first meeting and the dislike grew with every encounter. Kate found Mattie to be weak and simpering, falling back on her headaches to manipulate others. Although Kate herself might have been considered an alcoholic, she saw in Mattie's addiction to laudanum only weakness.

Mattie loathed Kate's loud abrasive manners, her drunken and unrestrained temper tantrums. She saw her as one of the lowest classes of prostitute, behaving more like a man than a woman. Oddly, of the two women, Kate was the one who had been raised in a wealthy, respected family from Europe, while Mattie was an orphan who had been surviving by her wits since she was thirteen years old.

At the end of summer 1879, Wyatt heard from his brothers, Morgan and Virgil. They were urging him to join them in Tombstone, Arizona, site of a large silver discovery. He made up his mind that he would be on a train before the year was ended whether Mattie chose to go or not. Mattie finally agreed to move to Arizona and join the Earp family, thinking it would allow her to finally be rid of Doc and Kate and their influence over Wyatt. Wyatt didn't tell her that Doc and Kate were also going to Tombstone and would meet the Earps there at a later date.

Once the decision was made to go to Arizona, Wyatt could talk of nothing else. On the evening before their departure, Wyatt was making his final rounds of a town he'd grown heartily sick of. Crates had been packed and marked and moved to the Santa Fe Depot where they sat waiting to be loaded onto the westbound train headed toward Las Vegas, New Mexico, where Wyatt expected to stay a few days while he arranged for a wagon to transport the couple and their belongings overland for Tombstone.

In late August 1879, on his last night before leaving Dodge City, Wyatt made a circuit of the plaza. Things were relatively quiet. The cattle season was winding down and cowboys were beginning to head back to Texas. Nevertheless, the saloons and dance halls remained open and lamplight spilled out on to Dodge City's streets. The wind blew in gusts, moving dirt and debris across the plaza. Wyatt noticed a dust devil form, grow and disappear.

Wyatt moved toward a loud argument going on in one of the saloons. As he'd already guessed, the arguing pair were Doc and Kate, having one of their famous public disputes. When Wyatt entered the saloon, a crowd had formed around the pair at a card table in the back. Cards and money had been swept off the table as had a broken whiskey bottle. Doc sat holding his crystal whiskey glass still half full. Kate, screeching at the top of her voice, stood over him. When she tried to knock the glass out of Doc's hand, he shoved her back.

"Darling," he drawled, "this may not be the finest whiskey, but let's not waste it."

As Wyatt moved toward the drama, he saw Kate pull a knife from the folds of her dress. She was lethal with a knife, the equal of any man in the room, even Doc. She advanced on Doc but was lifted off her feet by Wyatt who had approached her from behind; in Wyatt's opinion the only way to approach a poisonous snake. Wyatt did not like Kate, thought she was bad for Doc, but he kept his mouth shut on this matter.

Wyatt was strong and fast. He took the knife out of Kate's hand and had dumped her on the floor before she could catch her breath. "You sit there, Kate," he said, "or I'll haul you to the pokey." He turned to find his drunken friend was holding a small pistol in his face. He shoved Doc's arm up and took the pistol as Doc slumped back coughing blood into a linen handkerchief. Hoisting his friend to his feet and giving Kate a warning look, he led Doc outside where he promptly dumped the smaller man into a horse trough.

"God damn you, Wyatt!" shouted Doc with what breath he had left. He stood spluttering and spitting out the filthy water.

"You should know better than to pull that little pea shooter on me," said Wyatt. "I'm probably the only friend you've got on this earth." He put out a steadying hand as Doc hoisted himself out of the tank and collapsed onto a nearby bench.

"You're right, Wyatt," said Doc, sobered up by the dunking. "I should have had a bigger gun."

Wyatt sat beside his friend. "Wouldn't have mattered," he said, "my hide is thick."

They sat in the dark, contemplating their friendship and troublesome women. Doc nudged Wyatt's arm and pointed down the street. The wind had picked up, blowing a cloud of dirt toward them, as a dark shape at the center of the cloud kept pace, loping toward them. The men stared, mesmerized as a large black wolf approached them, seeming to grow larger as it neared. It stopped briefly to stare at the two friends then disappeared with the wind,

"Well, I'll be God damned," said Doc in a low voice. "Did you see that?"

"Yeah, I saw it," said Wyatt in a flat voice.

"You've seen it before," stated Doc.

"Yes," said Wyatt, "but before you ask, I don't know what it is except to say it's evil and it's been following me for over ten years."

"And now I've seen it, too," said Doc. "Guess that means we're going to die."

"We're all going to die," said Wyatt, "but this thing takes the ones you care about first."

Chapter 17
On the Move

When Mattie and Wyatt reached Las Vegas, New Mexico in September 1879, Wyatt noted that it felt just like being back in Dodge City and that wasn't what he wanted. After a brief stay to visit with old friends and secure a wagon to complete their overland journey, the Earps moved on to their final destination. He noted that there were a lot of people that he had known in Kansas.

Tombstone was only a small mining community when Wyatt and Mattie arrived. Without a rail line the town was remote and travel was by coach or wagon. Virgil, Morgan, and their wives had already arrived and set up housekeeping. While Wyatt and his brothers looked for business opportunities, their wives created homes.

Wyatt found the place surreal. In a year's time, the place grew by leaps and bounds with wealthy businessmen sharing the town with miners, Cowboys, ranchers and others of a lower class. There was a sharp divide between the groups, and the Earps, as lawmen, were on the fringes of the upper class. Wyatt mused that had he chosen a different profession, Doc would likely have been squarely placed in that upper echelon. He was well-dressed, well-educated and well-spoken, but he drank too much, led the life of a gambler, and he killed people.

Not long after the Earps arrived a troupe of players got off the stage in Tombstone, booked to perform at one of the popular venues providing theatrical entertainment. Among the troupe was a rather charming and mysterious young woman known as Josephine Marcus. As Wyatt watched, she stepped from the stage coach, her hand in Johnny Behan's.

"Well, Wyatt!" said a familiar voice behind him, "fancy meeting you here!"

Wyatt turned to see a smiling Doc Holliday watching him. "Doc," he said, "it's good to see you." He frowned slightly as a beautifully dressed woman stepped up and put her hand on Doc's arm. "Kate," he said, tipping his hat.

"Ah," said Doc, "I forgot you two already know each other! How Lovely!"

"Considering that I pulled her off of you to prevent her from slicing you into ribbons, one would think you'd remember that I know Kate," laughed Wyatt.

Doc smiled, "Ah, yes! I was a little tipsy at the time and it's slipped my mind. I hardly think my dear Kate would have sliced me to ribbons, though."

The look in Kate's eyes challenged either man to say more. She said, "I'm tired dearest; let us go to our rooms."

Remembering that Kate had known Wyatt in Wichita as well as in Dodge City, Doc's good humor evaporated and he turned surly and sarcastic. "So, my two best friends are also friends," he said.

"Doc," chided Wyatt, "don't be that way! Why don't we go let you beat me at a game of cards?"

Good humor returning, Doc smiled, "*Let* me? My dear boy, you don't have a choice! Maybe later. We need to get settled."

It became apparent early on that Mattie and Kate were never going to be friends. Kate always stayed by Doc's side while Mattie stayed home and fumed, waiting for Wyatt. The angrier Mattie got, the worse the headaches got. Most nights Wyatt arrived home in the predawn hours to find her passed out from the use of laudanum. When Wyatt tried to get her to seek help, she grew angry and spiteful.

While the troupe of actors was in town, Wyatt and Doc decided to take their wives to see what the group had to offer. As usual, Kate and Mattie were kept apart and Doc and Wyatt ended up talking over Mattie, who took exception to it.

Wyatt settled back to watch a Shakespearian reading and sat forward abruptly when the actor removed the mask and plumed hat to reveal Josephine Marcus; he was a she and a very pretty she at that. Wyatt stared and Mattie pouted.

At the intermission, the group rose and filed out. The men left the quarrelsome women and stepped outside to get some air. The two friends stood on the edge of the board sidewalk looking out over the darkened town, the flickering lamplight highlighting windows here and there.

Suddenly Doc said, "What are you going to do about Mattie?"

"What are you talking about?" responded Wyatt, knowing full well what Doc was referring to.

I am talking about Mattie and that very attractive actress," Doc said. "Mattie couldn't help but notice your obvious stare when the mask and hat came off."

Before he could stop himself, Wyatt bitterly said, "Mattie is so full of laudanum most of the time, she scarcely notices anything." Wyatt glanced over at Doc. "I shouldn't have said that. I can't leave her. She depends on me."

Doc sat quietly considering what Wyatt had said, "I understand more than you think, old friend."

The two men leaned against a post and surveyed the moonlit night. As they stared out into the darkness, a shadow glided down the street. Wyatt looked up expecting to see a cloud passing over the moon, but instead saw the shape of a large bird with a wingspan greater than the largest eagle he'd ever seen. "Hey, Doc, you seeing what I'm seeing?" he asked.

Doc nodded and his head turned as he saw the thing turn and glide back their way. There was shooting down the street and the men assumed it was some of the locals taking shots at the creature. The shooting was followed by angry shouting and a scream.

Wyatt said, "Maybe I'd better go see what's happening. Would you mind seeing Mattie home? Hopefully you can keep those two wildcats apart." That said, Wyatt strode off toward the continuing shouts and gunshots. Doc shrugged and re-entered the theater.

When Wyatt arrived on the scene outside one of the saloons, he saw Curly Bill in an extreme state of intoxication taking potshots at the moon while some of his Cowboy friends tried to calm him down. Marshal White was standing to one side hesitating. When he saw Wyatt approach, he gave a visible sigh of relief and called out.

"Wyatt, what should we do to get his gun away from him? I'm afraid he's going to shoot someone if he continues like this," said the marshal.

Wyatt would always remember what he advised and was eternally sorry for that advice. "He trusts you, Marshal," said Wyatt, and he doesn't trust me. If I keep you covered, do you think you can talk him into giving up his gun?"

Marshal White stepped forward calling out to Curly Bill, "Bill, I don't want to see anyone hurt and I know you don't want that either. Will you give me your gun and let your friends take you home?" He took another step forward, hands out to show that he was unarmed. "C'mon Bill, let's call it a night."

Bill turned and stared at the marshal. "Sure Marshal. I'm kinda tired anyway." He held his gun out and Marshal White stepped forward to take the pistol, butt first.

No one could say for sure what happened then. As the marshal took the pistol it was fired, striking Marshal White, who fell to the ground. Wyatt rushed forward, took the gun, calling for his brother Virgil to help him tame the gathering crowd. He took hold of Curly Bill who was standing staring down at the marshal.

"Marshal White!" he cried. "I didn't mean to! I didn't mean to!"

Wyatt took Bill's arm and the shotgun Virgil handed him and fired into the air. "Stay back! I'm taking this man into custody to await a verdict on what's happened here tonight." When some of the Cowboys surged forward, Virgil warned them to stay back and let the law take its course.

Curly Bill was taken to the jail and put under heavy guard until he could be taken to Tucson the next day for the hearing to determine if there was intent to kill or a drunken mistake.

As Virgil took over, Wyatt walked toward home thinking sadly about the marshal and reflecting that trouble just followed him everywhere he went. Reflecting on what he and Doc had seen previous to the incident, Wyatt was convinced the creature had been a forecast of the coming death of the marshal.

(Later in his life, Wyatt would learn that the giant bird-like creature had been spotted on a number of occasions and given the title the "Tombstone Thunderbird". A group of ranch hands had even reputedly shot it down and held it stretched to its full wingspan by eight men while a photograph was taken.)

Chapter 18
A Town On Edge

After the killing of Marshal White, the Earp brothers took a more active role in law enforcement in Tombstone, dividing the town further. Although Curly Bill was acquitted of the killing of White, the Cowboys continued to cause trouble in and around the area. It became obvious that Sheriff Behan was not going to do anything about it. The Cowboys were good for business even if it was largely business based on ill-gotten gains.

Things were further exacerbated by the town's two newspapers at complete odds with one another and practicing a high degree of yellow journalism on both sides. The *Epitaph* was a firm supporter of ridding Tombstone of corruption and what the editor called "the county ring" that included his dim view of Sheriff Johnny Behan. He made his feelings well known, believing that Behan was firmly on the side of the Cowboys and the criminal element.

On the other side was the *Weekly Nugget,* a pro-rancher, pro-Cowboy, and pro-Behan newspaper that stood firmly against the Earp family and their efforts to clean up the town. Naturally the two newspapers were continuously at war with one another seeing who could outdo the other in big headlines and exclamation points.

Sitting at a table near one of Wyatt's faro games, Doc watched idly as one Cowboy and miner after another lost money to the dealer and walked away disgruntled. Things turned ugly when a drunken Ike Clanton showed up. Everyone knew Ike, knew he had a violent temper when drunk, and knew him to be a liar of the first order. Doc sat up and took notice, sensing trouble was coming. As Ike's game came to its end, he began shouting and threatening, claiming he'd been cheated.

Wyatt spoke up, eyeing the man with disgust, "I've been sitting right here the whole time. You weren't cheated, you're just too drunk to play. Why don't you go home and sleep if off?"

Suddenly a pistol appeared in Clanton's hand. "You aint't gonna cheat me," he screamed. "I'll get you! We don't like the law around here!"

A look of surprise appeared on his face. He'd been so focused on Wyatt, Ike hadn't noticed Doc move up behind him.

Knife held firmly against Ike's neck, Doc said quietly, "Get out. Go home or bleed."

Wyatt removed the pistol from Clanton's hand and gave it to the bartender. "Next time you come in here, check all of your guns in with the bartender." Wyatt directed a hard look at the bartender as he said this, suspecting the man hadn't wanted to tangle with Ike.

When Clanton continued his belligerent tirade, Virgil Earp was called on to intervene. "You got some trouble here, Wyatt?"

"Ike's getting a little drunk and disorderly," said Wyatt. "He probably needs some time in the pokey to sober up."

With insults and protests, Clanton was led away. His guns remained in the bartender's care until he sobered up enough to return and claim them. Standing unnoticed in a dim corner of the room, Johnny Ringo watched the action. A friend of Ike, he didn't like what he'd witnessed and said something in Latin.

Doc turned sharply, replying in kind. Johnny smiled, shrugged his shoulders and left. "We have a mystery man among us," drawled Doc. "He is an educated man who speaks Latin as fluently as I do. I don't like him."

As the night drew to a close, Wyatt and Doc strolled down the quiet streets headed for their residences. Doc suddenly stopped and looked around him. "Do you feel it, Wyatt?" he asked. "There's something wrong with this place."

"What do you mean, Doc?" answered Wyatt, also looking around.

"I feel like there's some sickness here. What town calls itself 'Tombstone' for God's sake?" Doc paused and then said, "There's a miasma that hangs over this place and people seem to be afraid of something unseen and unnamed."

"Are you afraid, Doc?" asked Wyatt.

"Me?" exclaimed Doc. "What have I got to be afraid of? Death? I'm already half dead if you haven't noticed. What about you, Wyatt? What are you afraid of?"

"Nothing!" declared Wyatt. "Nothing except the darkness."

"That black shadow," stated Doc matter-of-factly, "I don't know what it is, but it's been just on the edge of my vision for quite some time." Doc considered. "And maybe it's just death waiting in the wings for me to die."

"Yeah," said Wyatt," but it doesn't seem to be out to kill me, only to hurt me by killing the people I care about. It's out there to do me harm and make me suffer. Is it Satan?" Abruptly, he changed the subject and said, "You know Morgan has got this crazy idea that at the time of our death, we'll see a bright light ahead of us?"

"A bright light?" laughed Doc. "How drunk was he when he was talking about this? And what if you're destined for Hell? I'm sure the gates of Heaven won't be open to me. I was raised in the Catholic Church. I haven't been inside a church since my mother passed. But I was raised to believe that if I would just go in and confess my sins to the priest, the doors to Heaven would open to me. You believe that?"

"Well, I guess I do," replied Wyatt. "The New Testament tells us that God loves us and if we believe, all is forgiven."

The two friends grew silent as they continued to stroll toward their lodgings. In the near distance a drawn-out howl cut through the night air raising the hair on the backs of their necks and they walked faster.

Chapter 19
The Gun Fight

Wyatt began to think that Doc might be right about Tombstone. There was something almost frantic about this town. He saw his job as black and white; either you obeyed the law, or you broke it. If you disobeyed the laws, you were a criminal subject to arrest and prosecution, but it didn't seem to be that way here.

The Cowboys, including Behan, saw the Earps, especially Wyatt, as over-zealous lawmen who were in the way of their criminal enterprises. A campaign of vicious rumors about the Earps, aided by the *Weekly Nugget* and others making money off lawlessness, began to circulate. These rumors accused the Earp brothers of robbing stage coaches and trains, killing innocents and skimming money from the local economy. Ike Clanton, fool that he was, seemed to be at the head of it all.

Wyatt tended to ignore it and go about the business of chasing down criminals and generally enforcing the law. Virgil was worried about the rumors but he was city marshal and perhaps it affected him more. Morgan, the youngest, and a favorite among the Earp family, was just a big happy-go-lucky kid. Doc was worried, too, as tensions continued to get worse.

October 26, 1881 things reached their breaking point. A drunken Ike Clanton was going all over town making threats, waving his pistol and generally priming his friends and enemies alike for a showdown. People began complaining about him and Sheriff Behan refused to involve himself. It was the city marshal's job, he told anyone who asked.

It fell to Virgil to confront Ike and insist he give up his weapons, leave town, or be arrested. In a vacant lot near the OK Corral, Ike and his companions appeared to be collecting their horses, preparing to leave town. Virgil was a smart man and certainly knew better than to confront the Cowboys alone. He took Wyatt, Morgan and Doc to disarm Ike and the other Cowboys with him.

Sheriff Behan ran up and grabbed Virgil's arm as he walked down the street. "I've already disarmed them," he shouted in an apparent attempt to delay the lawmen.

Virgil shook him off. "You've had your chance to uphold the law here and you've failed, so get back!"

Others shouted out as the foursome passed. "Be careful! Them Cowboys are armed!"

They came within view of Ike and his group. "Give up your weapons!" shouted Virgil.

And the shooting started. Virgil went down, then Billy Clanton. Ike came running like a crazy man, grabbed Wyatt's arm.

Ike shouted, "I'm unarmed! Don't shoot me!"

Wyatt thrust him aside, never taking his eyes off the action, focused on the job at hand. Then Morgan was wounded and the McLaury brothers died in the hail of bullets.

When it was over the only ones unscathed were Wyatt and Doc. Johnny Behan decided to step in and play the lawman and attempted to arrest Wyatt.

"Not today," said Wyatt and shoved Behan aside and walked over to check on his brothers.

That should have been the end of it, but that night Wyatt dreamed of worse to come.

Chapter 20
Violence Begets Violence

In reality, violence begets more violence and the troubles in Tombstone only worsened. People on all sides were appalled by the violence and killings in their midst. Now Tombstone's problems became drama that the whole country was talking about.

Between October and the end of December 1881, tensions mounted. Ike Clanton continued his campaign against the Earps, seemingly unaffected by the violence that had gotten his younger brother killed. He told anyone who would listen that they had started the trouble that ended near the OK Corral with three deaths including the death of his brother, Billy.

It seemed like the very air of Tombstone was throbbing with anger and desire for revenge on the part of the Cowboys and their friends. It had a terrible effect on Mattie whose headaches were worsening; she told Wyatt she felt as if the air around them was heavy, creating pressure in her head.

Doc's condition was worsening and he took to his bed while Kate tended to him, making dire predictions about his death. Doc had finally heard enough and ordered her out of the room, shouting "Don't come back in here with your foul gypsy predictions!" which ended in a fit of coughing so bad a doctor was called to his bedside. Once again Kate took up her position beside him.. This time, she kept her dire predictions to herself.

On the night of December 28, 1881, the violence exploded again. This time it was a sneak attack on Virgil Earp under cover of darkness. The load of buckshot that hit his left elbow was serious and there was talk of amputating the arm.

As Virgil lay in his bed fighting for his life, his wife tended to him, Christmas came and went. There were no celebrations for the Earp family. January and February came and went as well, but as March showed signs of spring trouble began again. Severe weather boiled up with rolling thunder and brilliant lightening displays that left the air crackling. Rain came down in buckets further unnerving the citizens of Tombstone who were not used to such weather.

Wyatt was on constant alert. Rumors of another attack on him or his family were making him nervous and he was trying to talk them into leaving Tombstone and moving on to California.

Before heading back to their lodgings late on the night of March 18, 1882, Wyatt and Morgan were playing a desultory game of pool. One of Morgan's dogs began to bark as lightning streaked across the sky and thunder boomed, causing the air to pulsate with pressure. The dog barked and growled aggressively as though something frightening had entered the room. Shots came from outside, breaking windows and hitting Morgan in the back. As he sank to the floor, a sound of someone running away was heard. The dog's barking turned into a long-drawn-out howl of distress.

Enduring extreme pain as the doctor probed to remove the bullet in his back, Morgan smiled up at Wyatt, gripped his wife's hand and said, "I see it, Wyatt, and it's coming to take me home. That bright light..."

The weeping widow fell to the floor, the dog howled mournfully, and Wyatt stood over his beloved younger brother's bloodied body and cried out, "Justice will be served over this one way or another! As God is my witness I will have my revenge!"

There were no arrests in the shooting of Virgil and Morgan Earp and Wyatt was done with Tombstone and its skewed system of law and order. He put his family on the train for California, and told Mattie he would see her again soon. He had some unfinished business that needed tending to and everything else would have to wait.

Rumors had reached his ears that another ambush was planned to catch Wyatt off guard as his family left town. One of the Cowboys approached with a tale so horrible Wyatt scarcely believed it. This informant drew the line at killing women. He'd stepped away, risking his own life when he told Wyatt that an ambush was planned to wipe out the entire family, women included.

Calling upon Doc to act as back-up, Wyatt planned an ambush of his own. Doc had recovered from his latest attack of consumption, weak but on his feet again. An argument with Kate had sent her packing raging that she would leave Doc for good.

Two angry men stood on the platform of the new depot and watched as the train pulled out bound for California. Except Wyatt, all of the remaining Earp family was on the train. Kate was there, too, with a new man on her arm, dealing one more thrust of the figural knife to Doc's heart. Turning aside, they searched among the trains and crowd at the station for the ambush party. Things had not gone as Wyatt expected and he feared the information had been incomplete. One step ahead, though, he expected some trickery and had men loyal to the cause of justice sitting and waiting for Cowboys to attempt an ambush on the train several miles out of Tombstone.

Now these two friends would look Death in the face and begin a dangerous game of hide and seek until Wyatt was satisfied his vendetta against the Cowboys was fulfilled. They had hurt his family, Morgan was dead, and the Cowboys were going to be wiped from the face of the earth if Wyatt had anything to do with it. The black shadow crept closer, reaching out to take his soul and he knew it was there, one more thing he had to defeat.

A determined Wyatt rounded up his posse of trusted friends, deputized them and let the Cowboys know that Hell was coming for them and there would be no more playing by the rules for Wyatt. His honor was in shambles and he was just like any other outlaw now. He didn't think he would ever be going back into the law-and-order business.

Chapter 21
Vendetta Ride

For nearly a month, Wyatt Earp pursued his sworn enemies in a vendetta ride that would become legendary. He was a man on fire blazing with anger and hatred against the men who'd done his family so much harm. Not since Urilla died years before had he felt so lacking in the calm self-control that he had always prided himself on. This time there was a target the life-and-blood men who had performed the foul deeds, and he could do something about them. He could send them to hell.

As his enemies fell one by one and men around him died, Wyatt remained unscathed. In the end he abruptly quit and with his posse moved into Colorado, out of reach of his enemies and Arizona law. Now he was just tired and empty. He had largely forgotten Mattie. He had intended to join her, had intended at least to write her a letter. But when Wyatt didn't show up, Mattie disappeared back into her life as a prostitute. She finally died of an overdose of laudanum. She was another victim of the dark shadow always hovering over Wyatt.

He had a falling out with Doc Holliday as well, and the two old friends parted ways on angry words. When Doc was arrested for a killing in Tombstone, Wyatt stepped up and enlisted the help of Bat Masterson to get him freed. Their paths were largely separated after that.

During this dark time in Wyatt Earp's life, amid reports in Tombstone that he was dead, he felt at the lowest point in his life since the death of his beloved Urilla. The demon that had been pursuing him for years now seemed to have Wyatt firmly in its grip, suffocating him. He saw its shadowy form in his dreams, caught glimpses out of the corner of his eye, and faced it in the mirror when he was shaving. *What have I become?* he wondered morosely.

Wyatt continued to defend his actions to himself during this low period, telling himself that he had gotten justice for his brothers in the only way left to him. The court system in Arizona had failed him and his family when it failed to apprehend his brother's attackers, failed to prosecute on technicalities, and released guilty criminals on false alibis provided by other criminals. He was no longer a lawman who believed justice would be served under the law, but had become jaded and lost his faith in what was right under the law.

Wyatt had never forgotten the actress, Josephine Marcus. In Tombstone he'd had a dalliance with her but vowed to stay with Mattie, a woman who clearly needed him. Josephine just as clearly did not need anyone. There were always men around and her family's money to provide for her every want.

So a year later Wyatt Earp reunited with Josephine in San Francisco. He thought the dark days were behind him. He even managed to forget the shadow that had been hanging over his life since he'd first encountered it. After he'd found Josephine, their lives took on an erratic routine of adventuring, bouncing from one boom town to another always looking for the streak of good luck that would make them wealthy for the rest of their lives.

While in a restaurant in Colorado, Josephine looked up with an exclamation. "Look who's here!"

Wyatt looked around to see a much frailer Doc Holliday moving toward them, the same old devil-may-care smile on his face.

"Why, Wyatt, I do declare!" drawled Doc. "How the hell are you?" He turned to Josephine and tipped his hat, ever the debonair Southern gentleman. "Ah, the beautiful actress, Josephine Marcus. How delightful."

This last remark gained him a spiteful smile from Josephine who replied, "It's Mrs. Wyatt Earp now."

Doc bowed slightly and said, "Delightful!" But his glance at Wyatt said something else.

Wyatt squirmed a little bit knowing Doc was questioning his abandonment of Mattie. "It's good to see you, Doc," replied Wyatt. "What are you doing in Denver?"

"Oh, you know, living the high life as always!" smiled Doc. "A little cheating at cards here and a little gambling there. You staying here in the hotel?"

"Yes," said Wyatt, smiling at his wife, "Josie likes her room service."

"I'm staying here as well," said Doc. "Join me for dinner?" He saw Wyatt glance at his new wife for an okay and inwardly winced.

Josie spoke, "That would be lovely, Doc."

The dinner was all about old times, two gunmen now largely in different circumstances. Doc's health was still declining as it had been for over twenty years. Wyatt was largely past the days of being a lawman in rough towns. Doc was always looking for the next card game. Wyatt was looking for a lucky strike that would make him rich. In spite of reminisces, it was a merry evening. Doc didn't mention Kate and Wyatt didn't bring her up. Water under the bridge.

All of them had had plenty to drink and Josie jokingly admitted to Doc that her family were descended from gypsies.

Doc didn't miss a beat and stuck out his palm. "Well, madam," he drawled, "will you do a reading?" He smiled impishly at Josie, knowing it would both flatter her and piss her off.

Wyatt frowned. "She was only joking, Doc."

"Oh, I don't think she was!" exclaimed Doc. I'm betting your fair Josephine has the sight and I demand a reading. A betting man will always take a bet." He winked at Josie.

Josie sat forward. "Okay, then, Doc," she said, "let's see if my mother's old stories have a bit of truth in them." Josie took Doc's soft hand in hers, preparing to act the part of a fortune-teller. At first she appeared to study Doc's hand, gently tracing the lines of his palm. She shut her eyes. "I see a man with..." Suddenly Josie's eyes flew open and she looked straight at Doc, eyes slightly unfocused, surprise on her face. "I see your death," she whispered dropping Doc's hand.

Wyatt sat forward his body tense. "You saw something? What did you see?"

Josie looked first at Wyatt and then at Doc. "I saw you in a bed, Doc, in a hospital with Wyatt beside you. There was a Catholic priest there, too, giving last rites, but you were smiling."

"Smiling?" queried Doc.

"Yes," explained Josie, "you'd told Wyatt that you had been making your confessions – long overdue – to the priest. You closed your eyes. Then you opened them and said, "I'll be damned! Morgan was right.""

Is this a true reading?" asked Doc with a note of suspicion in his voice.

"Yes," said Josie, "I believe it is and Wyatt will be there with you."

Chapter 22
Life After the OK Corral

After Wyatt felt he had done what he had set out to do by punishing those responsible for the maiming and death of his brothers, life went on for Wyatt and Josie. But it all ended almost as quickly as it had begun. If he had been asked to describe how he felt Wyatt decided the word 'deflated' would apply. He was no longer a man on fire fueled by the anger and disappointment he felt over an inadequate system of justice that had failed his family again and again.

Then Wyatt got the telegram from Bat Masterson in Trinidad, Colorado. There was trouble in Dodge City and the old Dodge City gang was needed to intervene on behalf of one of their old friends, Luke Short. Leaving Josie in Denver, Wyatt headed for Dodge City.

In Wyatt's typical style, he managed to end a confrontation between two parties well-known to him from his years as a lawman in Dodge City. At the end of the dispute, he sat down with old friends to have a picture taken. Someone jokingly referred to the group as "the Dodge City Peace Commission."

Although Luke Short won his war with the law-and-order faction that had taken over in Dodge City, he was still essentially run out of town and moved on to Fort Worth, Texas. For the next ten years Luke Short and his young wife, Hattie, traveled between Texas, Kansas and Chicago, involved not only in gambling but the saloon business and horse racing. Luke died in Gueda Springs, Kansas, hoping the mineral waters there would cure his heart problems. They did not.

After Luke Short's problems in Dodge City were cleared up, Wyatt decided to hang around for a few more days, seeing old friends and waiting to receive his own copy of the photograph of the "Peace Commission."

One night as he stood outside the Long Branch Saloon, smoking a cigarette and staring up at the night sky, he heard a small cry. He looked around but the lamplight that provided the glow by which card games were played, did not extend far outside of the windows and doorways. To see clearly along the dark boardwalk and dirty streets, Wyatt would have needed a torch. When he didn't hear the sound again, he settled back against the wall of the building.

The cry came again, this time a little louder and as Wyatt turned in the direction of the sound, he felt something move past him swiftly toward the cry. He smelled that distinctive odor he would never forget. Suddenly, he was running, his eyes able to see more clearly. He felt then as though he was seeing through someone else's eyes. His hearing became sharper and he heard the whimpering that he hadn't detect before. Then Wyatt saw the helpless shape lying against a wall in an alleyway and knew what was about to happen as the young woman, battered and bloodied, looked up in relief that quickly changed to fear. He saw but was powerless to stop what was happening before his eyes. Fleetingly he wondered if he was involved.

His cigarette had burned down in his fingers and a terrifying scream came, bringing him back to an awareness of his surroundings. He realized he was standing where he'd been when he felt the thing pass him. What, then, had he experienced? He looked around to see men pouring out of saloons along the street, lanterns held high and guns tightly gripped in hands that shook slightly. Somewhere in the small crowd he heard someone say something that surprised him.

Wyatt turned sharply, "What did you say?"

Worried faces stared back at him, fear in their eyes. Finally, someone in the back spoke up. I said, "Another one?" The man didn't identify himself.

Wyatt decided not to press the issue, but led the group of men forward, taking a lantern from a man next to him. "This way," he said, "the scream came from the alley."

They surged forward and found what Wyatt had expected to find. He caught sight of a large black dog disappearing into the darkness but no one else appeared to see it. He suspected there were several others who'd seen this level of viciousness before. And he wondered how often the creature used Dodge City as a feeding ground.

The hapless young woman, most surely one of the lower class of prostitutes who used the ill lit alleyways to ply their trade, lay on her back. She was horribly torn and mangled as though a large animal with sharp teeth and claws had attacked her. The smell of sulfur lingered in the air but no one except Wyatt appeared to notice it.

He heard a soft growl behind him and turned sharply to see a pair of eyes, red and glowing in the dark. In his head he saw the vision through those red eyes as he used his teeth to tear at the soft white flesh using large claws to tear the clothing away. He shuddered wondering if the beast had possessed him for a moment.

When the doctor had come and removed the body, Wyatt returned to the Long Branch and ordered a drink. As he sat there at the bar staring into his whiskey a man he didn't recognize leaned against the bar beside him.

"You ever seen anything like that before?" the strange man asked.

When Wyatt looked up he saw it was the man from the crowd who'd spoken up about the previous attacks. "Yes," he said. "Sounds like you have, too."

"I seen it plenty out in the mining camps in Colorado," the man said. "Ugly business."

"But you've seen it here, too?" asked Wyatt.

"Once or twice," admitted the man, "especially during the height of the cattle season when no one is really noticing."

"You have any idea what's doing this?" Wyatt asked now, watching the man closely.

"Some mighty big animal," the man answered. "Some think it's a cowboy doing the killing, but I don't think so. It's something a lot darker than a drunk cowboy."

"Have you seen something?" asked Wyatt.

"Something kinda like a big black wolf," the man replied, turning now to look Wyatt in the eye. "You may as well go on home and get some sleep. He won't strike again tonight."

As the man lifted his hat and nodded his good-bye, the lamplight fell across his face. Wyatt could have sworn the man's eyes glowed red.

Chapter 23

Coeur d' Alene, Idaho 1884

Josie and Wyatt arrived in Idaho intent, once again, on striking it rich in the new town of Coeur d' Alene. This time Wyatt's brother, Jim, joined them and their new business venture unfolded – literally. The brothers purchased a large round circus tent, fifty feet in diameter, calling it a dance hall. Later they opened the White Elephant Saloon. It wasn't long before Wyatt was once again in the law enforcement business in addition to everything else.

The mining town, like most others, was full of men seeking their fortunes doing rough, dirty, hard work. When their work days ended they turned to the few entertainments available to them. First, they drank and they gambled, then they got rowdy. A few disappeared in the bordellos beginning to spring up. Some drunks got happy, singing, clapping, stomping their feet with any musical entertainment that might be offered. Others grew maudlin, missing families and not striking it rich as they'd hoped. And many grew angry and mean as they drank the strong, cheap whiskey.

Disputes erupted, mostly over claim jumping, and Wyatt and brother Jim were frequently called upon to settle things before someone got killed. One particularly ugly dispute was over a town lot. With bullets flying between the two angry combatants, Wyatt and Jim stepped in the middle of the fray. As bullets whistled past them the brothers grew calm and joked with one another about the poor marksmanship of the two parties. Finally the local sheriff arrived to help end the free-for-all.

Jim had that family trait, that admirable calm in the face of danger. Like Wyatt, he simply responded, trusting he would live through it all. The problem, though, as Wyatt saw it in some of his more somber and reflective moments, was that two of his brothers had been shot and one had died. Virgil had that same calm demeanor but had been caught off guard, ambushed, and the Cowboy had paid for that.

But Morgan, he was always the jittery one. He always stepped into a fight as readily as the rest of them, but that trait that Wyatt and Jim had seemed to have skipped Morgan. Wyatt was always calculating the odds, and these days, it was an automatic response he wasn't even conscious of. His eyes were always moving, seeing his chances against first this man and that, calculating the weapons and the amount of ammunition an opponent might have. He always played the odds.

Wyatt felt blessed to be alive but at the same time felt guilty about it. Was his life protected and preserved by that unknown darkness at the expense of his loved ones? It was a hard thing to consider – that he was responsible in this abstract way for those losses. As he somberly considered these painful thoughts, he felt the darkness close in on him. He thought he saw the dark shadowy form in his peripheral vision. And he felt Morgan's presence keenly, laughing at him for feeling so guilty and sad.

One evening Wyatt stood outside the saloon, enjoying the air outside the hot smokey rooms. It had been humid all day. If Mattie had still been with him, he thought that she would be suffering one of her headaches. Only twice had he heard some harsh words over the way he'd treated Mattie; one of those shaming him was Doc, the other was Virgil. He knew his behavior toward Mattie had been shameful but that didn't alter the fact that he felt responsible for her death as well.

As he stood there lost in thought, keeping an eye on the darkening sky to the west, he felt the approach of the storm. The wind had shifted direction and was bringing drier air and a storm with it. He saw the flash of lightening, heard the distant thunder and thought about the night Virgil had been shot. There had been a storm then, too.

He continued to watch the storm move closer and felt rather than heard someone move up beside him. Assuming it was Jim, he turned to comment on the approaching bad weather. But it was not Jim who stood there; it was another brother, the one who had been dead for over three years.

"Wyatt," said Morgan, "how you holding up?"

"Morg," said Wyatt softly, "is it really you?"

"Remember that night?" Morgan asked. "It was a night like this one. There was a lot of lightning and thunder. We felt that storm coming all day."

Wyatt stared at the apparition beside him. "If you're real, then why are you here? This isn't Tombstone and we've all mourned you for these past three years."

"But you never learn, do you?" hissed Morgan. "You let Virgil down, you let me down and now your reckless disregard for life is going to get Jim killed, too. Why didn't you protect us, brother? Why didn't you see it all coming? I should be standing here beside you right now, alive."

Wyatt hung his head and said softly, "You don't think I haven't felt the guilt over your loss? God damn it, Morgan! I feel the weight of your death every day!"

The sound of boots on the wooden boardwalk came from behind Wyatt. He looked around to see Jim coming toward him. The spell was broken and Morgan was gone.

"Who you talkin' to, Wyatt?" asked Jim.

Wyatt tried not to look embarrassed as he laughed and said, "Myself, I guess. Didn't realize I was speaking out loud." He laughed again and said, "People are going to think I'm losing my mind if I keep that up."

As he said this, he looked back over his shoulder. He could still see Morgan faintly, his eyes glowing red as he disappeared with a small pop and a sizzle that smelled faintly of sulfur.

Chapter 24
Glenwood Springs

Five years went by before Wyatt received a summons from a sanitorium in Glenwood Springs telling him that John Holliday was asking for him to come. It had been a long stretch of normalcy for Wyatt. He began to think the shadowy creature, if it was real at all, had gone.

Doc continued on with his life after his meeting with Wyatt and Josie in Denver, spending most of the time he had left in Leadville. In spite of his failing health, or maybe because of it, he was no less dangerous a man. He shot a man over a gambling dispute in 1884. Kate reappeared, and dedicated herself to nursing her beloved Doc even after he entered the sanitorium expecting to live out the rest of his life as consumption continued to rob him of his ability to breathe.

When Wyatt arrived it was to find his friend bedridden and in a deep discussion with a Catholic priest. Kate was dismissed during these daily discussions. Although she, too, had been raised in the Catholic faith, Doc felt she was too frivolous to be included in the serious conversations they had.

Wyatt maintained a respectful silence as Doc concluded his time with the priest. Once the holy man left the room, Wyatt drew up a chair and remarked, "You think God is going to save you after the life you've led?"

Instead of meeting Wyatt's remark with a sarcastic reply, Doc admonished his friend saying, "I am not, as you so glibly put it, expecting God is going to bring my life back and make my afterlife pleasant. I do, however, want to know what awaits me." He eyed Wyatt, waiting for a reply. When none was given, he said, "Don't you ever wonder what's next?"

"No," said Wyatt, "I don't guess I do. I just take each day as it comes. When my life is over, then it's over. Morgan kept talking about some mumbo jumbo before he was murdered, saying something about tunnels and bright lights."

"That's the problem with you, Wyatt," said Doc, "You have no imagination. However, I don't think you imagine that darkness that hovers around us. You seem to be the only one besides myself who has seen it."

"And what's that, Doc?" asked Wyatt, knowing exactly what Doc was talking about and dreading the conversation.

"I want to know what we have in common that we have this black shadow around us all the time," explained Doc. "I want to understand what it is."

"What does the priest say?" asked Wyatt, loath to talk about the thing that had largely left him alone for the last five years.

"I have discussed such beings in a very general way with my priest," said Doc. "He's the one that actually brought the topic up for discussion. He asked me why I thought my room always appeared to be so dark and shadowy. He noted how the darkness always receded into a particular corner of the room when he came in only to return when he left. I was surprised that he saw it, but he assured me he was well aware of the presence of evil."

"Is he saying that you are evil?" asked Wyatt.

"No," said Doc. "He's warning me that this thing is waiting to take my soul when I die."

"Is that what you think?" asked Wyatt.

Fighting to stay awake Doc asked Wyatt to come back the next morning. "I want to know what connects us, Wyatt," said Doc. "I want to know of your experiences."

Day after day Wyatt sat at Doc's bedside. He told his friend all he could remember about the stories around the campfires at night, how he encountered the creature that was alternately dark and wolf-like or dark smoke. He told Doc bitterly about Urilla's death and his own descent into lawlessness. Finally, he said, "You know, Doc, I have been damned lucky. I'm still alive, never even felt a bullet or a knife touch my flesh. But the losses I've suffered have damned near broken me." He looked at Doc and asked, "So, how did you first encounter this dark thing?"

After a long silence, Doc said, "You know, Wyatt, I feel like my life has been cloaked in shadows since my youth. I was utterly devoted to my very Southern mother. She died of the consumption when I was only fifteen years old. In my loneliness I turned to my cousin, Mattie, whom I loved to distraction. We could not marry, however, and she entered a convent." Doc paused realizing that his cousin did not know of his approaching death. "Wyatt, you must promise me that you will notify Mattie of my death and ask her to pray for my soul. Promise me!"

"Of course I will, Doc," Wyatt soothed. "Where shall I write her?"

"I have her letters among my personal effects. You will find everything you require." Doc's voice trailed off.

"You're tired, Doc," said Wyatt. "We'll talk some more tomorrow."

"No! Stay a little longer!" exclaimed Doc. "I haven't told you how I encountered the dark shadow you were telling me about." He paused to gather his thoughts then went on. "My upbringing was much different than yours, you understand. We were a wealthy family, we had slaves, and I was an only child with a sick mother. I had a devoted Mammy who looked after my every need and told me stories at bedtime. These people were very superstitious, you have to understand, and the stories she sometimes told seemed very unlikely to me. On one occasion, though, I had not behaved well toward my mother who had her good days and her bad days, and Mammy came to me and began to scold me. I got sassy with her and she engaged my father to discipline me for the misbehavior. I guess no one understood that I was just a young boy who was puzzled and frightened about my mother's illness. My father consigned me to my room and sent Mammy up to make sure I stayed there. She began to tell me stories of the dark creatures that came to lurk in the night and took bad people away forever. She was very graphic in her descriptions, listing the names of people who had disappeared from our home and never returned."

Wyatt noticed that Doc's speech was becoming slower and his breathing more labored. He interrupted saying, "Doc, we can finish this up tomorrow."

"No, I'm almost done and I feel sure that I will not be here tomorrow," Doc said. "This is my last chance to unburden myself to you.

Wyatt nodded his understanding and said, "Okay, then, go on, but I will be here tomorrow no matter what."

"Those stories my Mammy told didn't scare me for long, as you might imagine." Doc gave a weak smile and went on, "When I was fourteen I grew irritated with a group of negros I found swimming in the "whites-only" swimming hole. I ordered them out but they didn't leave. I went back to the house and got one of my father's pistols, so heavy I could barely control it and I ordered them out again, this time with the gun leveled at them. They scrambled to leave then but I fired anyway, only meaning to fire a warning shot so they would know I meant business. I killed one of the boys. I got into a great deal of trouble with my family over this, not because I killed someone, but because I killed a boy who was a valuable worker, a piece of property. As punishment my Mammy was taken from me and I was forced to look after myself. A year later my mother died and soon after that my dear Mattie entered the convent, leaving me with literally no one who cared about me. My world darkened then and has remained dark ever since."

"Our stories are not at all the same," remarked Wyatt. "You killed someone and drew attention to yourself. I was curious and my curiosity led me to an encounter with something evil and dark."

"Perhaps the similarity is in the lesson," said Doc. "In some way, we drew negative attention to ourselves and it has plagued us all of our lives."

Doc was visibly weakened by the long conversation and Wyatt rose to leave. "You get some rest now," he said, "and I will be back tomorrow."

When Wyatt returned to continue their discussion the next day, he noted the date was November 8. He arrived to find the priest, Father Downey, delivering last rites, Kate sobbing quietly nearby. Doc reached out with his thin, frail hand to take his friend's hand in a grip so light Wyatt wasn't sure his friend was even still alive.

In a whisper, Doc said, "I'm done, old friend." He smiled. "I see that light Morgan talked about and I'm getting closer. I fear we won't be able to continue with our conversation unless I find a way to reach out to you from my afterlife. Take care, Wyatt." Doc's hand fell from his grip, but Wyatt could swear he still felt Doc's grip on his arm, young and strong.

Chapter 25
After Doc

Doc's death hit Wyatt harder than he had imagined it would. Doc had long been a constant in his life, a loyal friend even when their paths didn't cross for months and even years. While he in no way felt guilty about Doc's passing, he somehow felt left behind. Wyatt knew that in spite of Doc's battle to stay alive, his death from consumption was inevitable. He had admired Doc. He wasn't sure himself how he would have handled the life sentence his friend had been given at such an early age. But Doc didn't sit in some fancy room in his family's home and play the invalid. He lived his life and, by God, when someone threatened to take his precious life, they ran the risk of paying the ultimate price. With Doc it was always kill or be killed.

July 3, 1888 Wyatt received word that Mattie had died. Everyone had lost track of her until word of her death was passed along. She died by her own hand of a laudanum overdose either by accident or by suicide. Once again he mourned the loss of someone who'd once been important to him, and once again he felt overwhelming guilt because he'd not only abandoned her, he'd forgotten his promise to her. How could he consider himself a man of honor and integrity when he'd treated so helpless a creature so cruelly? It preyed upon him and he wondered if that dark shadow had been responsible for her death. Had it appeared beside her whispering in her ear? Had it told her the best way to take her revenge for Wyatt's treatment of her was by destroying herself?

During this time, America began seeing newspaper headlines about gruesome murders in London, England. Wyatt read these reports with interest and a feeling of dread. Were these murders being committed by the same dark thing that dogged him? Certainly, they were vicious in a way that seemed to indicate this to be so. Were they being committed by someone Wyatt knew or had met? He racked his brain feeling there was a connection that he was missing. But try as he might the memory remained elusive.

When the Jack the Ripper murders abruptly ended and there were no arrests or even suspects in the cases, people began to speculate that Jack the Ripper was not an Englishman at all, but someone who had been visiting England. After all, people said, if it had been a foreigner who had left the England then the murders would naturally have stopped. There were a lot of theories.

Wyatt read these speculations with interest. Then similar murders began to occur in the United States and newspapers jumped on the vague information, fueling the idea that the Ripper was now on American soil. One newspaper known for its sensationalism began to air the theory that Jack the Ripper had been in America before, that he was a world traveler, and committing heinous crimes wherever he went.

Still, some small thing niggled at the back of Wyatt's memory. Who or what was it? Someone he knew? Somewhere he'd been? Some incident he'd witnessed? The memory simply wouldn't come and he finally put the fruitless thoughts aside, but the image of a dog kept occurring to him.

He dreamed of the dog, a fine slender animal that could run fast enough to catch an antelope. He saw the dog barely touching the ground as it ran and he heard a man's voice calling to it, urging it to bring down the prey. When the dog finally subdued the antelope, the man beside him praised the dog and walked toward it, pulling a long slender blade from a sheath hanging from his trousers. As Wyatt watched, the man pushed the dog away and pulling the dying creature's head back by its antlers, he gave one quick swipe, slitting the downed animal's throat.

Wyatt woke with a gasp and said, "Dog!"

Chapter 26
Who Was Wyatt Earp?

Since his teens Wyatt Earp had known he was not like others. He had always been a quiet man, strong and determined to move forward no matter what obstacles stood in his way. Men trusted him and women found his quiet unsmiling countenance appealing. Those who knew him and liked him thought him a loyal, trustworthy man of integrity.

But there was another side of Wyatt Earp that hid behind the calm unflappable demeanor. He had the clinical mind of a cold-blooded killer and when he determined someone was to die, he spared no mercy. His heart was as cold and hard as a marble tombstone.

Some people saw only the best in Wyatt Earp. His brother, Virgil, saw the dangerous side of Wyatt. For Doc Holliday, Wyatt was not only a friend, but a best friend and the two never wavered in their recognition and admiration of one another.

And Mattie, poor Mattie, she loved and depended on Wyatt, the man who continually supplied her with laudanum. She saw too late that the man she loved was slowly killing her and watching her die with cold indifference. At first, he thought her pretty and entertaining but he soon grew bored with her shrewish manner and lack of self-control. As she swallowed the last dregs of liquid from that little brown bottle, her only friend when the headaches began, she heard Wyatt's calm voice telling her that it was all right, that if she'd just surrender to the drug, it would all be over. No more headaches, no more worry about a future with a man she'd trusted. And no more troubling guilt for Wyatt Earp.

As for Josephine Marcus, she was fun, funny, and kept him entertained. He might grow angry, or exasperated with Josie, but she constantly surprised him, never bored him, and they moved through life companionably. Not at all like the clinging Mattie.

Whether or not Wyatt actually contributed to the suffering and deaths of friends and family members, he felt guilt about them. In his teens, during his time in the railroad and mining camps, Wyatt was simply curious about stories he heard about the disappearances of workers. Instead of assuming, like management did, that workers had run off, he believed the fanciful tales of the workers. Statistics, though, were on the side of management who knew from experience that a certain number of workers were bound to leave the job. The idea that there was some foul beast out in the darkness killing workmen was laughable.

Wyatt knew that he had shot some living thing that first night so many years ago. There was evidence of that although he never found a body or a wounded man. He tried to convince himself he had shot a deer, but it was more interesting to give himself over to the stories told around the camp fires.

Chapter 27
Ripper Murders

As Wyatt grew older, he began to reflect on past experiences. He had put the whole episode out of his mind during periods of normalcy. His marriage to Urilla was one such normal period. Wyatt and Urilla had been happy together and they were expecting their first child. He knew, though, that people suspected him of murdering her. He had been home at lunch time; people had seen him. He remembered she was fine when he left for work. She had voiced some vague fears, but Wyatt had put all of that talk down to her pregnancy. Still, people reported hearing raised voices. Others said he'd been vague and unresponsive at the city jail when they'd stopped by to chat or raise a concern. He remembered none of that. All he did remember was realizing it was about time for his shift to be over when he heard feet running past the open door of the jail. Someone yelled, "Wyatt! Come on! Your house is on fire!"

He did remember running recklessly into the burning house and looking for Urilla. He remembered holding her as she lay dying on the soft grass. She was barely alive but told him she'd lost the baby and there was a lot of blood. Virgil had commented on it.

After Urilla was buried and Wyatt had been cleared of any charges, he still felt people's eyes follow him and whispers start up behind his back as he passed by. He entered a period of deep depression. He asked himself again and again if her death was his fault, but how could it have been? The mental conversation played in his head on a continuous loop. Growing desperate from guilt, alcohol, and lack of sleep, Wyatt finally left Missouri behind and entered a period of manic activity, digging a hole he wasn't going to escape if he couldn't get some control over his feeling of guilt and helplessness.

Sometimes Wyatt felt like he was seeing things that weren't there. He had never been much of a drinker and he wasn't an opium user. There were no explanations for some of the things he'd seen. Was the smell imaginary, too?

Once free of his misdeeds in Oklahoma Territory Wyatt had begun to gain his equilibrium. He considered himself to have a strong moral code, but his enemies were more likely to point to his strong sense of self-preservation and ability to convince himself he was right and they were wrong.

Wyatt had managed to convince himself that there really was some dark creature that was after him. And the events in London between 1888 and 1894 cemented his convictions. The newspaper accounts of a vicious mystery killer who focused on prostitutes of the lowest order in the poorest part of London had Wyatt wondering how many of the dark creatures there might be in the world.

Chapter 28
James Kelly

Dark forces continued at work in Dodge City, Kansas many years after Wyatt Earp left that city for the last time. As long as the cattle trade brought cowboys, gamblers, prostitutes, and other disagreeable elements to Dodge City, the darkness remained for the hunting ground the nocturnal atmosphere of the place provided.

The creatures of the night, those that were human, acted much as the dark creatures themselves did. They slept by day only coming to life when the lamps were lit. The young cowboys who never appeared to sleep provided the perfect distraction for the grisly murders of a few prostitutes. No one appeared to notice the frequency or the similarities of the killings. The women were only lowly prostitutes, after all.

By 1885, Dodge City had begun to change. Law abiding citizens with families wanted schools, legal businesses lining the streets, and safety from the criminal element that arrived in town every summer with the cattle trade.

When the dead line was moved to the Colorado border, favoring farming over cattle, Dodge City changed almost overnight. Instead of saloon-owning mayors, lawmen involved with the gambling crowd, and interests that favored and attracted cattlemen and cowboys, there were honest businessmen using Kansas' dry state laws to get rid of the lawless element and make an honest living.

Abruptly, a man named James Kelly was out of business. He had been Dodge City's mayor there for a number of years, from 1877 until 1881, but had lost his seat to the progressive anti-alcohol, anti-cowboy, anti-gambling crowd. He invested heavily in real estate, losing much of his wealth after 1886. Fires destroyed buildings and a blizzard destroyed cattle herds, leaving him nearly penniless. Reflecting morosely on what lay ahead for him, Kelly had decided to take what was left of his fortune and return to Ireland to visit the place of his birth one final time.

Kelly arrived in England several months later, having sold his racing hounds and his horses. He found lodging in the meanest part of London, getting his drinks for free in the dark dirty pubs because of his story-telling skills. It seemed no matter where he was, people wanted to hear stories about the cattle days in Dodge City. Even the prostitutes were accommodating.

When he began to feel unwell, developing night sweats and weight loss and a troubling cough, Kelly began to drink more heavily, walking the filthy streets at night until he felt he could sleep.

His loud, boisterous personality deteriorated into depression and anger. Finding himself in front of a doctor's office one day, he stepped inside, hoping to find relief from the chronic cough. The doctor, already drunk at ten a.m., asked him several pointed questions, listened to his chest and told him bluntly that he had the consumption. He handed him a bottle of laudanum and demanded payment.

Bitterly angry and blaming the prostitutes for his contraction of the dreaded disease, he stumbled along the streets in a blue mood clutching his pocket where the bottle was placed. Entering his miserable room, he sat on the edge of the dirty cot and sipped from the bottle.

The results were nothing short of miraculous! Kelly felt as though he'd been released from some tight, confined space. He was able to take in a deep breath without coughing. The ache in his chest dissipated and he found himself relaxing for the first time in many months. He lay back on the filthy bedding and dozed off.

He woke hours later to find he'd knocked the precious bottle over and half of the elixir was gone, soaked into the rough floorboards by his bed. He felt despair sweep over him again as he looked at what was left, carefully stoppering it to save the remaining few ounces. It was growing dark and he determined to go out and find a source for more of the precious laudanum.

He went back to the doctor who had given him the laudanum, but the man was out on a call. He turned then to an apothecary shop but in this mean and dirty part of town he had no success in acquiring another bottle.

In his desperation, Kelly was becoming increasingly angry. The tightness in his chest and the coughing worsened. When he spotted a gaudily dressed woman leaning against a pub wall sipping from a small bottle, he walked purposefully toward her and demanded to know what was in the bottle.

She quickly tucked it into her bodice and with a defiant look declared the bottle was none of his business. "You can buy me services, though," she said with a saucy look.

He shouted at her, "I'm not interested in you, stupid woman! I'm interested in obtaining some laudanum."

An avaricious look appeared in her eyes and she asked, "What'll you give me fer it then, luv?"

"Where do you get it?" he demanded.

"Oh, no you don't!" the woman snarled. "You can pay me fer it if you want it."

With uncontrolled rage, Kelly grabbed the woman, tore her bodice and thrust his hand into her dress, fumbling for the bottle. As he extracted the precious drug amid her loud protests, he shoved her to the ground and threw a couple of coins at her that struck the pavement. They bounced and landed on her skirts. He quickly walked away.

As Kelly swigged greedily from the bottle it occurred to him the woman would never reveal her source now. He began to calm down, reasoning that if a lowly whore could get a ready supply of laudanum, then surely he could, too. Should he try approaching more doctors or apothecary shops?

He returned to his room, lay down, and relaxed. The drug had ended his fits of coughing and calmed his anxiety. He determined that the next day he would see the doctor again to get information about obtaining the drug that would ease the effects of the consumption and make his life more bearable.

Upon rising the next morning, he reached for the bottle, now carefully stoppered, and took a small sip. By the time he had performed his morning ablutions and dressed, the effects of the opiate were spreading through his body, calming him down and offering hope.

Returning to the doctor he'd visited two days before, his illness was again explained to him and he was given another brown bottle. This time, however, he had the presence of mind to question the doctor further about obtaining this medication that calmed the coughing and aching chest.

The doctor stared at him in surprise. "Good Lord, man!" he exclaimed "Have you never used opium or its various mixtures before?"

Kelly said, "No, doc, I've always been a whiskey drinker. Never touched the opium."

"It will be your friend, now," explained the doctor, "as long as you can control your use of it. If you don't, it will kill you before the consumption does," He went on to tell Kelly the places he could replace his prescription, and there were many of them, it being the popular drug of choice.

James Kelly had always been an intemperate man. He would risk everything on the turn of a card, the speed and skills of his dogs, on a speculative business deal. Mostly, he lost, but it had never bothered him in the past. Until now, with life running out and under the influence of tinctures of opium, Kelly grew increasingly angry when he drained the last dregs of one of his bottles. He had taken to lining them up on the floor around the edges of his room in a fit of wry whimsey.

Sometimes he counted the bottles, wondering at the sheer number of them, all drained. He didn't even remember many of the passing days as he navigated the streets of London in a stupor. He felt some mild alarm on occasions when he'd wake to find himself covered in blood spatters. Once he ascertained it wasn't his blood, however he soon forgot about it, and discarded the bloodied clothing, simply buying or stealing another set of clothes.

By the end of 1891 James Kelly had managed to get his addiction under control as the consumption went into remission. He decided he was ready to return to the United States. Maybe he'd go to Chicago, visit the Columbian Exposition.

Chapter 29
Wyatt and Josie Go To The World's Fair

Leading their nomadic life, Wyatt and Josie decided a trip to Chicago would be great fun. They would visit the World's Columbian Exposition, take in the sights of the city and meander south to St. Louis. They'd go see some horse racing, place a few bets, and have a good time. Josie loved living in good quality hotels, ordering room service, and trying out the finer restaurants. Her mother had seen to it that she had a fine set of fashionable new clothes to take on whatever Chicago had to offer.

The couple had a whale of a good time in spite of the trouble experienced during the six months of the fair in 1893. Wyatt and Josie were generally not affected by the darkness hovering over the event.

A small pox epidemic was accelerated and spread across the country by the crowds of people attending. Over seven hundred fifty thousand people showed up on opening day and the crowds grew increasingly larger with everyone coming to see the electric light city.

However, the World's Columbian Exposition, a celebration of Christopher Columbus's discovery of a new world, was a huge success celebrating and showcasing the United States as never before. Electric lights were a big feature of the exposition, enabling two teams to play a football game at night.

All in all, the Earps enjoyed themselves immensely. As the fair drew to a close, people were horrified when Chicago's popular mayor was assassinated. Surprisingly though, all these troubles surprisingly left Wyatt untouched until the newspapers began to announce multiple disappearances of young girls. He felt a familiar chill accompanied by a hovering darkness over the fairgrounds for the first time since they'd arrived. He sensed some evil, something he would know when he encountered it.

On the street just outside of the exposition grounds one day, Wyatt recognized a familiar face from Dodge City. He hailed the man, who turned and with a smile on his face, moved toward the couple.

"Wyatt Earp!" exclaimed Dog Kelly, "what a sight for sore eyes!" The two men shook hands vigorously.

Wyatt turned, and taking Josie's arm, urged her forward. "This is my wife, Josephine," said Wyatt proudly. Pleasantries exchanged, Josie wandered toward the women's exhibits while Wyatt and Dog Kelly leaned against a fence and visited, catching up on personal and Dodge City history.

"What are you doing in Chicago, Dog?" asked Wyatt. "You racing some of your dogs or horses?"

Dog Kelly had always been a greyhound owner, sometimes keeping over one hundred dogs. He raced them around Kansas at Great Bend and Abilene or whatever temporary track became available for running and wagering.

"No, I sold all my dogs," said Kelly sadly. "Even sold my horses," he said mournfully.

"What?" exclaimed Wyatt. "Dog Kelly without dogs or horses? This is news."

"I was diagnosed with consumption," explained Kelly, not entirely truthfully. "I decided to travel to Ireland and England, seeing the old places I once knew." A coughing spell interrupted him and Wyatt could see he wasn't in a good way.

"I'm real sorry to hear that," said Wyatt, placing a hand on his old friend's shoulder. "If you're not here to race your animals or visit the World Exposition, what are you doing in Chicago?"

"Well, that's kind of a long story, but if you want to join me for dinner this evening, I'd be happy to tell my sad tale," replied Dog Kelly.

Looking around for Josie, Wyatt waved her over. "The mayor will be joining us for dinner tonight," he said. With a twinkle in his eyes, he remarked, "I expect you'll need a new dress for the occasion?"

"Oh yes," she replied, nodding in his direction with a broad smile on her face. "We'd be honored to dine with you this evening. I don't think we've ever met, but I do know you by reputation. And you can admire the new dress my husband has insisted I buy." They all laughed.

It was agreed that the former mayor would join the Earps for dinner in the beautifully appointed dining room at the hotel where they were lodging.

As they walked away, Josie turned to Wyatt and said, "Did you notice Mayor Kelly's strange expression when I remarked that I knew him by his reputation?"

Wyatt denied that he'd seen anything, but added that the man he'd known in Dodge City was much changed from the man they'd just encountered. "Dog Kelly was always a jovial Irishman who loved his dogs and horses," remarked Wyatt, taking Josie's arm and guiding her through the crowds of people. "He has a daughter somewhere, but the girl's mother died some years ago. I wasn't aware that he'd left Dodge City, but I guess we'll hear about it this evening."

Chapter 30
Kelly According to Kelly

Darkness had fallen and lamps were lit when Dog Kelly strolled into the hotel dining room where Wyatt and Josie were seated at a conveniently private table in a far corner of the large dining room. Spotting the elaborately dressed Josie, Dog waved a hand in greeting and walked to their table bypassing a maître d'hôtel.

Shaking hands with Wyatt, removing his hat, and bowing slightly toward Josie, the former mayor of Dodge City took a seat. Flipping open the snowy white napkin and laying it on his lap he looked around. "Lovely place," he remarked.

Wyatt smiled fondly at Josie and said, "Josie does know how to choose well! And she loves her room service!" Everyone laughed then picked up their menus and began to look them over, discussing this offering and that. When a waiter approached they had made their choices and gave them to the waiter, starting with the lady at the table who was very specific. The men gave their order more quickly, then they all sat back to wait, chatting animatedly.

"I didn't even know you'd left Dodge City," remarked Wyatt. "Of course, we've been out West and don't hear much from Kansas anymore."

"Once the do-gooders took over and I was out of the mayor's job," began Kelly, "it wasn't a very friendly place anymore. I decided I had a desire to see my homeland once again, so I sold everything, went to pay my daughter Irene a visit and took off."

"Are you staying in Chicago now?" asked Josie.

"I bought some land and built a new rooming house," replied Kelly. "As soon as I returned from England I heard about this giant fair in Chicago and saw a business opportunity. I figured if there was land within easy walking distance of the Exposition grounds, I'd see if I could acquire it and build a place for visitors. Figured there was money to be made. It turned out to be a good decision. I figured when the fair was over if business slowed down, I'd just sell it and move on."

What will you do when you're ready to leave here?" asked Wyatt.

I've decided to return to Dodge City," said Kelly, grinning. "Maybe I'll just run for mayor again as a straight business man."

Wyatt raised his eyebrows in surprise. "After they practically ran you out of there?"

"I'm a new man," replied Kelly. "They won't even know the new me." He sat quietly for a few seconds, then said, "And, I'm trying to get myself admitted to the Fort Dodge Soldiers Home," Kelly admitted. "Turns out, I have to get special permission, so I've written some letters and I'm waiting for confirmation that they will accept me. I'd like to live out the rest of my life among a few old friends where there's someone to look after my needs as this damned disease gets worse."

"That makes sense," replied Wyatt. "You think you can get a good price for your rooming house?"

"Absolutely," said Kelly emphatically. "I plan to take my profits and get as far away from the big city as I can. And the sooner the better! It surely won't be as profitable once this fair is over, but I expect it will stay full of lodgers all the same. Chicago is growing."

Talk drifted to the food, the good old days in Dodge City, and Wyatt's and Josie's adventures as the evening wore on. Kelly remained quiet during most of the conversation his eyes wandering over the room.

As the friends parted ways at the end of the evening, Kelly remarked, "Wyatt, you should come see my building. I'll give you a tour. If anyone you know is looking for a business opportunity, you can tell them you know a place that will be available for purchase anytime. Are you interested?" Dog gave Wyatt a peculiar little smile as he said this.

"No, old friend," replied Wyatt, "Josie and me, we like the west coast. We spend our winters in town and summer in our mining camps in Arizona. Chicago is too damned cold for us."

Kelly just shrugged, acknowledging the expected answer. "But you'll come for a tour tomorrow?" he prodded. "Say, after lunch?"

"Sure, Dog," said Wyatt, "I'd like to see it."

The men parted ways on the promise. Wyatt was wondering why Kelly was so anxious to show the place off. But he shrugged and strode forward to catch up with his wife, who window shopped as she waited.

Chapter 31

An Interesting Investment

Wyatt returned to the front entrance of the Columbian Exposition after lunch the following day. Josie had declined to come along, saying she'd rather do some personal shopping. That was fine with Wyatt, who hated shopping.

Soon, Dog Kelly appeared, greeting Wyatt cheerfully. "So, you came," he said.

"I said I would," replied Wyatt a little testily. "You know I keep my word."

"Yes, yes, you always did," replied Kelly. "Come this way, it's just a few blocks. There's no use finding a cab." He turned and headed back the way he'd come away from the Exposition, Wyatt striding along beside him.

Dog was right. In spite of the sheer size of the Exposition grounds, his rooming house was well-placed to appeal to those working at or attending the fair for a length of time. Looking at the three-story building, Wyatt admired Dog's business acumen in seeing and acting upon such an opportunity.

Kelly stood in front, arms spread and said, "What do you think?" He watched Wyatt's expression as he took it in. He noticed his friend's brief puzzled look before Wyatt blinked, erasing his expression and appearing to view his surroundings with calm appreciation.

"I'm impressed," said Wyatt, but he stood his ground not making a move to enter the building and see the interior.

"Come in," exclaimed Kelly. "You've got to see the inside, too." He was already pulling a large front door open, waving Wyatt inside.

Wyatt squared his shoulders, but experienced a feeling of something wrong even before he crossed the threshold. Carefully arranging his facial features to reveal only neutral interest, he looked around him as Dog led him through the entire building except the basement.

When he asked about the basement, Kelly shrugged it off saying, "Nothing down there but a heating system and storage for tenant's trunks."

Wyatt asked the appropriate questions any interested friend might ask, but he thought Dog sensed his confusion and uneasiness. That in itself seemed kind of odd. Why would he feel this unease and why would Dog seem to expect him to?

Wyatt asked, "You only take female boarders?"

"Oh, yes," replied Kelly. "Women are much better boarders than men. They're rule-followers, see? I post strict rules and most obey. If they don't, one of the other boarders will let me or the matron know. I hire matrons to live here to help me keep the place orderly. I can't do it all myself. I don't allow no men nor booze in their rooms, either. Makes for a safe place to live and rooms are rented as fast as they come available.

"Why would you even have any empty rooms with all of the care you've put into this place?" asked Wyatt.

"Some girls get homesick and return home," said Kelly. "One of them got married a while back. You know, women are flighty creatures!"

Wyatt stepped outside, casting another glance at the building and still concerned over something. "Thanks for the tour, Dog, "he said. "You want to join us for lunch?"

"No, I have some things I need to see to." Kelly smiled and moved away.

As Wyatt walked back toward his hotel, he puzzled over what was bothering him. There was something sad, but at the same time chilling about Dog's the place. For such a new place, there was a slight smell that wasn't pleasant. It wasn't the odor of cleaning, but of something else. A rooming house as well kept as Kelly's appeared to be would require hired labor to freshen walls with paint, woodwork with polish, and rugs sprinkled with damp tea leaves and briskly swept to remove dirt. One could expect the scents of vinegar, lemon, wax and soap, but the scents that Wyatt caught were something else. It came to him that what he'd smelled might have been sulfur and burning hair. In a time when women were curling their hair with hot irons, the smell of burned hair might not be unexpected, but the smell of sulfur certainly seemed out of place.

Through long experience in mining and railroad camps, Wyatt was fully aware of the smell of burning hair. It was not uncommon for men to move too close to campfires during a cold night, sometimes getting their hair singed. It wasn't unknown, either, for a drunk to stumble and fall into a fire.

The sulfur, too, was not an unfamiliar smell although it had been many years since he'd experienced it. In many mining and trapping camps distant from any settlement it was common practice to keep sulfur powder during the winter months. It was sprinkled liberally over a dead body which was wrapped tightly in canvas to reduce its deterioration until it could be buried or returned to family.

Through long experience in mining and railroad camps, Wyatt was fully aware of the smell of burning hair. It was not uncommon for men to move too close to campfires during a cold night, sometimes getting their hair singed. It wasn't unknown, either, for a drunk to stumble and fall into a fire.

Wyatt pondered these memories wondering why such smells would be evident in a relatively new hotel. Something dark and frightening was going on with his old friend, Kelly. But he kept walking. He didn't want to know. He never encountered James Kelly again.

Chapter 32

Boom and Bust

Wyatt and Josie settled into a life of boom and bust, an adventurous if sometimes poor existence. They frequently took up lodgings with Josie's family or any friends willing to have them for indefinite stays. Wyatt was always welcome; Josie often was not.

By the early 1900s, Josie had proposed that Wyatt write an autobiography. Surely, she reasoned, the public would pay good money for such a book. But as he aged, Wyatt's fame waned and times changed. Besides, he hadn't the ability to actually write about himself, he explained patiently to his wife.

She persisted, however, and they found a man to write a book about her husband's extraordinary life. The first book was ill-written, but it focused some attention back on Wyatt Earp, the Western lawman.

The interest came from an entirely new direction. Moving pictures were a growing industry and drew crowds into auditoriums and newly built moving picture theaters. Wyatt's life and exploits became interesting again to a whole new generation of people. While Wyatt's old friend and fellow lawman Bat Masterson preferred living his life out of the limelight, Wyatt reveled in the attention. And Josie saw opportunities to make money.

Wyatt began to visit movie sets, taking an interest in how the soundless moving pictures were made. He took Josie to see a two- or three-minute French film made in Paris showing a large steam engine barreling toward the camera as it entered the station. Produced around 1900, the only sound produced came from a small orchestra or an organ. It frightened Josie who rose from her seat and turned to run toward the exit. Wyat grasped her hand firmly and pulled her back explaining that it wasn't real but a strip of film on which the arriving train had been captured. It was spliced together and run through a device that showed the sequence in larger-than-life size on a giant screen.

Wyatt later took Josie to see The Great Train Robbery, a film he admired very much as it was very realistic in his opinion. It was this film that drove him to see how the filming was done and, if possible, meet the people involved.

In the meantime Josie, who fancied herself a poker player on the same level as her husband, became a constant gambler. She waited for Wyatt to leave the house, then boarded a trolley headed for the gaming parlors and race tracks. She lost again and again.

When Wyatt found out about her gambling he was angry and their already precarious living arrangements worsened. He ordered her to stop and when that didn't work, he made sure access to his money was restricted. But Josie had become possessed by some demon that drove her to gamble. The angrier Wyatt became, the more secretive and stubborn Josie got.

She begged money from her father, borrowed from her sister, and when they pressed her for repayment, she began to steal from Wyatt. She took a diamond tie pin, a gold nugget, and even his gold watch. When threatening men began to appear at the door to their home, Wyatt ran them off with a loaded shot gun, then turned to Josie and demanded all of the truth from her.

"You are not a gambler, Josie!" Wyatt said to her. "You are a terrible card player and worse at betting on horses because you like their names. No more gambling! We're practically out on the street now. And I got a note from your father demanding his money back."

Josie stubbornly insisted she'd just had a run of bad luck. Wyatt turned his back on her and went to their bedroom where he kept the diamond pin, expecting to pawn or sell it to pay his wife's debts.

When he returned to the kitchen where Josie sat, defiance now drained from her, he was white-faced, his anger barely in check. "You've resorted to stealing from me, now?" he said in a hoarse voice. "What else have you done for money?" The implication was clear and Josie blanched.

Josie looked at her husband and silently held out her hands to him. "I'm sorry, Wyatt. I was so sure I could win enough to cover my losses."

Wyatt turned and left without a word, letting the screen door bang shut behind him. Josie heard the car crank to life and head away from the house, the sound of the engine fading away. Then she cried. She wasn't a woman given to crying, but she had never seen her husband so angry with her. Many husbands would have struck their wives over a lot less, but that was not Wyatt's way. He would leave to sort everything out and return in a day or two.

When the second day passed and he hadn't returned, she grew frantic. Wyatt always came back. She began to think about how foolish she had been. She regretted the secretive gambling, but even as she thought these things, the urge to gamble was there. She held firm and stayed home waiting for her husband to return.

And he did return after a week away. Surprisingly, he even returned with the items Josie had so carelessly thrown away so she could place one more bet, play one more hand of poker. He frowned at her when she met him at the door.

He looked at her sternly and said, "Josie," he said, "I've put myself to a lot of trouble because of you. I've managed to pay your debts and redeem what you took without my permission."

Josie flinched, but did not say a word. She knew there was more to come from her normally taciturn husband.

Wyatt stared at her and continued, "I have instructed your family not to loan you another penny. I have settled with those two that came to our door and others like them. You put me in a bad spot. Luckily, I didn't have to shoot anyone. But I will shoot the next loan shark that loans you money and they all know this. You have been cut off. If you do this again, you will be on your own. Do you understand me? All I have left is my reputation and my word and you damned near ruined it."

Josie knew what Wyatt said was his final word on the subject. The darkness in his eyes was almost unbearable and she had been the cause of it all.

Chapter 33
Off to Hollywood

In a day or two the Earps' lives had returned to near normal. By week's end, Wyatt appeared to have made a decision.

"Josie," he said, "pack our bags. We're headed to Hollywood. I think you need a change of scenery and I need to earn some money."

Wyatt had done what he set out to do. With the help of an old acquaintance from their days in Alaska, he had met a man named Walsh, a film director. The acquaintance was Jack London whom he'd run into in a saloon while he was sorting out Josie's difficulties. Their talk of old times had turned to the silent film portrayal of the old days and London had taken Wyatt to meet the director.

As London and Earp talked to Walsh, word got around the movie set that Wyatt Earp had shown up. Even Charlie Chaplin had sauntered over to meet the legendary lawman.

Wyatt was again enjoying the life of a well-known and revered figure when in 1922 a scurrilous story appeared in the *Los Angeles Times*. It was a pack of lies, making the real hero of Tombstone Johnny Behan. Other stories began to appear as well and they rankled. Wyatt fumed about them, even going so far as to find one of the writers and insist on telling his side of the incidents.

But the film industry rolled on in spite of bad press, showing Wyatt Earp as the legendary lawman, a man of morals and principles. Wyatt met many young actors whose fame would rival his own, though only one was famous for what he'd actually done, and not the portrayals of what Wyatt had done.

His friend, William Hart, suggested Wyatt write a book about his life to counter all the misinformation, a tactic that had failed once. If anyone were to profit from it, it would be Josie. Wyatt would never see his book published.

Besides William Hart, Wyatt had become friends with many of the young actors wishing to hear his firsthand accounts of the Old West and practice his moves. The acting legend John Wayne was rumored to have modeled his own characters after Wyatt Earp.

Tom Mix was one who was fascinated by Earp's life, although Mix was creating some legends of his own. His cowboy stunt performances with his horse, Tony, wowed audiences on and off the screen. He had been part of such Wild West shows as the Millers' 101 Ranch in Ponca City, Oklahoma, and was a bartender in Oklahoma's territorial capital of Gutherie. He'd even been the night marshal in Dewey, Oklahoma. Mix was acting a past that wasn't his, but was just on the outer edge of the Wild West Era. In Oklahoma and Indian Territory, the Wild West lasted a bit longer, spilling into the moving picture age.

Wyatt liked Mix, although on the surface they appeared to be completely unlike one another. While Wyatt was quiet and steadfast in his beliefs, Mix was flashy and full of attitude, But Wyatt saw in Tom Mix some of the same darkness and confusion he felt himself. He longed to share his experiences, even ask if the actor had ever had similar experiences.

Over drinks in a bar near the movie set one evening, Wyatt Earp and Tom Mix swapped stories. Wyatt, a serious lawman and gambler in his lifetime, was curious about the life of a Wild West Show performer where the new style of cowboy displayed riding and roping skills, dressed in clothes he'd never seen the likes of before, and acted out an earlier, tougher lifestyle in well-pressed clothing.

Mix, on the other hand, was equally enamored of the hard riding, law-and-order versus cowboy gun battles on main street of Wyatt's experiences. As their conversation progressed Wyatt told Mix about his early encounter with the dark entity he'd seen nearly fifty hears before. He was taken aback when the younger man admitted that he, too, had such an experience out on the vast acres of the 101 Ranch. He'd been a working cow hand then. He, too, had heard rumors of men disappearing. And he'd seen the dark thing on other occasions. They saw the same darkness in one another's eyes, a well-hidden fear always held in check, always just beyond rational belief. What had they actually experienced? Neither had an answer. Wyatt confided Doc Holliday's similar experiences. Mix called to mind an old friend, also deceased, who had admitted to seeing demons.

After this conversation, the two men spent hours discussing and comparing what they'd seen, smelled, heard. Was it the product of imagination? Was it because they were a similar breed of man? Their discussions always ended with unanswered questions.

After one such session in 1929 Wyatt looked at himself in a mirror and saw only an empty space where his face should have been. He closed his eyes and looked again. Was this his demon playing tricks? But still he could not see his face in the mirror. He knew then that the aches and pains of old age were something more and that death was finally on his doorstep. He was eighty years old and had outlived all of his brothers. He had beaten death too many times, but it had caught up like it always did. He went to bed that night and dreamed of staring back in time, watching the years roll by then coming to a sudden stop in front of him. As he dreamed, a dark figure appeared to motion Wyatt forward. But he held back, refusing to accompany the featureless thing. Then someone else's life spiraled before him. He saw Tom Mix meet a much less peaceful end and wept for him.

Waking in the morning he shook off the strange dreams of the night before. He decided they were all due to his continuing discussions about darkness and evil with Tom Mix. He was feeling his eighty years this morning having just seen his last brother buried. He sat on the edge of the sagging mattress and for the first time in his life thought about just going back to bed, claiming the right of an invalid and staying there while someone looked after him for once.

He snorted in disgust at this feeling of weakness and pushed himself to his feet, swaying a little before pulling his clothes on and beginning his day. He saw by the look on Josie's face when he entered the kitchen that something really was wrong with him,

"Wyatt!" she screamed as he collapsed on the floor. He saw the dark figure from the corner of his eye, coming for him. He'd cheated death so many times. A bullet had never seared his skin nor entered his body during all the days as a lawman. No one had ever really manhandled him or beaten him senseless. He'd always held strong in his convictions that he made the right choices. He'd cheated death of its due for eighty years, but his time was up.

As he was pulled away, he heard Josie screaming, heard the neighbors arriving, heard people crying. At his funeral, Tom Mix, acting as one of his pall bearers, wept, sobbing quietly as the more stoic older men carried on.

Chapter 34
Epilogue

When Wyatt Earp left Dodge City, Kansas in 1878 the darkness continued to follow him, but evil is a universal thing and it also remained in Dodge City. It stayed, continuing to feed on the transient population of Dodge City by lamplight. It was already there when Wyatt Earp arrived and it remained after he moved on. It savored the cowboys whose names were unknown, the prostitutes that moved restlessly in and out of towns like Dodge City, and the gamblers, who moved with the money. When the cattle days were over, some of the darkness left, too. People knew one another. They knew if their neighbor was ill, if a churchgoer didn't show up, and if a faithful worker disappeared.

Darkness moved on with men like Wyatt, men who desired adventure and riches and even anonymity. It moved on with a tide of evil and men who simply didn't care, and it fed on the fleeting populations of the Old West.

Evil did not disappear with the Wild West. It changed and adapted. It hid in big cities where people didn't know one another and didn't want to. It lived anywhere people turned a blind eye to darkness.

Wyatt Earp knew this. He couldn't verbalize it. He couldn't make sense of it, but he knew it. He knew that evil existed in apathy and lack of care for others. It drove him to listen and believe and look for answers. It drove him to do what he thought was right no matter what others thought. Maybe other people had not seen the dark shadows hiding from the lamplight.

Wyatt Earp died at eighty years old never doubting he'd done what was right in the face of evil.

Other Books by Carol L. Jenkner

Road Kill O'Connor Series

Road Kill

Road Rage

Road Block

Armadillo Jack Series

The Armadillo Way

**About the Author**

Carol L. Jenkner is a retired teacher who continues to work as an educator at an area museum. She has published four previous novels. Her interactions with people she meets and the stories they tell are a constant source of ideas for her stories. She lives in a 1935 cottage with her three cats. She enjoys historical research, needlework, reading and attending estate sales and auctions.